The
A Brownie

AS TOLD TO MY CHILD
BY MISS MULOCK

·ILLUSTRATED·

Loki's Publishing

Contents

The Adventures of a Brownie

Adventure the First
Brownie and the Cook

There was once a little Brownie, who lived—where do you think he lived? in a coal-cellar.

Now a coal-cellar may seem a most curious place to choose to live in; but then a Brownie is a curious creature—a fairy, and yet not one of that sort of fairies who fly about on gossamer wings, and dance in the moonlight, and so on. He never dances; and as to wings, what use would they be to him in a coal-cellar? He is a sober, stay-at-home, household elf—nothing much to look at, even if you did see him, which you are not likely to do—only a little old man, about a foot high, all dressed in brown, with a brown face and hands, and a brown peaked cap, just the color of a brown mouse. And, like a mouse, he hides in corners—especially kitchen corners, and only comes out after dark when nobody is about, and so sometimes people call him Mr. Nobody.

I said you were not likely to see him. I never did, certainly, and never knew any body that did; but still, if you were to go into Devonshire, you would hear many funny stories about Brownies in general, and so I may as well tell you the adventures of this particular Brownie, who belonged to a family there; which family he had followed from house to house, most faithfully, for years and years.

A good many people had heard him—or supposed they had—when there were extraordinary noises about the house; noises which must have come from a mouse or a rat—or a

Brownie. But nobody had ever seen him except the children—the three little boys and three little girls—who declared he often came to play with them when they were alone, and was the nicest companion in the world, though he was such an old man—hundreds of years old! He was full of fun and mischief, and up to all sorts of tricks, but he never did any body any harm unless they deserved it.

Brownie was supposed to live under one particular coal, in the darkest corner of the cellar, which was never allowed to be disturbed. Why he had chosen it nobody knew, and how he lived there, nobody knew either, nor what he lived upon. Except that, ever since the family could remember, there had always been a bowl of milk put behind the coal-cellar door for the Brownie's supper. Perhaps he drank it—perhaps he didn't: anyhow, the bowl was always found empty next morning. The old Cook, who had lived all her life in the family, had never forgotten to give Brownie his supper; but at last she died, and a young cook came in her stead, who was very apt to forget every thing. She was also both careless and lazy, and disliked taking the trouble to put a bowl of milk in the same place every night for Mr. Nobody. "She didn't believe in Brownies," she said; "she had never seen one, and seeing's believing." So she laughed at the other servants, who looked very grave, and put the bowl of milk in its place as often as they could, without saying much about it.

But once, when Brownie woke up, at his usual hour for rising—ten o'clock at night, and looked round in search of his supper—which was, in fact, his breakfast—he found nothing there. At first he could not imagine such neglect, and went smelling and smelling about for his bowl of milk—it was not always placed in the same corner now—but in vain.

"This will never do," said he; and being extremely hungry, began running about the coal-cellar to see what he could find. His eyes were as useful in the dark as in the light—like a pussy-cat's; but there was nothing to be seen—not even a potato paring, or a dry crust, or a well-gnawed bone, such as Tiny the terrier sometimes brought into the coal-cellar and left on the floor—nothing, in short, but heaps of coals and coal-dust; and even a Brownie cannot eat that, you know.

"Can't stand this; quite impossible!" said the Brownie, tightening his belt to make his poor little inside feel less empty. He had been asleep so long—about a week, I believe, as was his habit when there was nothing to do—that he seemed ready to eat his own head, or his boots, or any thing. 'What's to be done? Since nobody brings my supper, I must go and fetch it.'

He spoke quickly, for he always thought quickly, and made up his mind in a minute. To be sure it was a very little mind, like his little body; but he did the best he could with it, and was not a bad sort of old fellow, after all. In the house he had never done any harm, and often some good, for he frightened away all the rats, mice, and black-beetles. Not the crickets—he liked them, as the old Cook had done: she said they were such cheerful creatures, and always brought luck to the house. But the young Cook could not bear them, and used to pour boiling water down their holes, and set basins of beer for them with little wooden bridges up to the brim, that they might walk up, tumble in, and be drowned.

So there was not even a cricket singing in the silent house when Brownie put his head out of his coal-cellar door, which, to his surprise, he found open. Old Cook used to lock it every night, but the young Cook had left that key, and the kitchen and pantry keys too, all dangling in the lock, so that any thief might have got in, and wandered all over the house without being found out.

"Hurrah, here's luck!" cried Brownie, tossing his cap up in the air, and bounding right through the scullery into the kitchen. It was quite empty, but there was a good fire burning itself out—just for its own amusement, and the remains of a capital supper spread on the table—enough for half a dozen people being left still.

Would you like to know what there was? Devonshire cream, of course; and part of a large dish of junket, which is something like curds and whey. Lots of bread-and-butter and cheese, and half an apple-pudding. Also a great jug of cider and another of milk, and several half-full glasses, and no end of dirty plates, knives, and forks. All were scattered about the table in the most untidy fashion, just as the servants had risen from their supper, without thinking to put any thing away.

Brownie screwed up his little old face and turned up his button of a nose, and gave a long whistle. You might not believe it, seeing he lived in a coal-cellar; but really he liked tidiness, and always played his pranks upon disorderly or slovenly folk.

"Whew!" said he; "here's a chance. What a supper I'll get now!"

And he jumped on to a chair and thence to the table, but so quietly that the large black cat with four white paws, called Muff, because she was so fat and soft and her fur so long, who sat dozing in front of the fire, just opened one eye and went to sleep again. She had tried to get her nose into the milk-jug, but it was too small; and the junket-dish was too deep for her to reach, except with one paw. She didn't care much for bread and cheese and apple-pudding, and was very well fed besides; so, after just wandering round the table, she had jumped down from it again, and settled herself to sleep on the hearth.

But Brownie had no notion of going to sleep. He wanted his supper, and oh! what a supper he did eat! first one thing and then another, and then trying every thing all over again. And oh! what a lot he drank—first milk and then cider, and then mixed the two together in a way that would have disagreed with any body except a Brownie. As it was, he was obliged to slacken his belt several times, and at last took it off altogether. But he must have had a most extraordinary capacity for eating and drinking—since, after he had nearly cleared the table, he was just as lively as if he had had no supper at all.

Now his jumping was a little awkward, for there happened to be a clean white tablecloth: as this was only Monday, it had had no time to get dirty—untidy as the Cook was. And you know Brownie lived in a coal-cellar, and his feet were black with running about in coal dust. So wherever he trod, he left the impression behind, until at last the whole tablecloth was covered with black marks.

Not that he minded this; in fact, he took great pains to make the cloth as dirty as possible; and then laughing loudly, "Ho, ho, ho!" leaped on to the hearth, and began teasing the cat; squeaking like a mouse, or chirping like a cricket, or buzzing like a fly; and altogether disturbing poor Pussy's mind so much, that she went and hid herself in the farthest corner, and left him the hearth all to himself, where he lay at ease till daybreak.

Then, hearing a slight noise overhead, which might be the servants getting up, he jumped on to the table again—gobbled up the few remaining crumbs for his breakfast, and scampered off to his coal-cellar; where he hid himself under his big coal, and fell asleep for the day.

Well, the Cook came downstairs rather earlier than usual, for she remembered she had to clear off the remains of supper; but lo and behold, there was nothing left to clear. Every bit of food was eaten up—the cheese looked as if a dozen mice had been nibbling at it, and nibbled it down to the very rind; the milk and cider were all drunk—and mice don't care for milk and cider, you know. As for the apple-pudding, it had vanished altogether; and the dish was licked as clean as if Boxer, the yard-dog, had been at it in his hungriest mood.

"And my white table-cloth—oh, my clean white table-cloth! What can have been done to it?" cried she, in amazement. For it was all over little black footmarks, just the size of a baby's foot—only babies don't wear shoes with nails in them, and don't run about and climb on kitchen tables after all the family have gone to bed.

Cook was a little frightened; but her fright changed to anger when she saw the large black cat stretched comfortably on the hearth. Poor Muff had crept there for a little snooze after Brownie went away.

"You nasty cat! I see it all now; it's you that have eaten up all the supper; it's you that have been on my clean table-cloth with your dirty paws."

They were white paws, and as clean as possible; but the Cook never thought of that, any more than she did of the fact that cats don't usually drink cider or eat apple-pudding.

"I'll teach you to come stealing food in this way; take that—and that—and that!"

Cook got hold of a broom and beat poor Pussy till the creature ran mewing away. She couldn't speak, you know—unfortunate cat! and tell people that it was Brownie who had done it all.

Next night Cook thought she would make all safe and sure; so, instead of letting the cat sleep by the fire, she shut her up in the chilly coal-cellar, locked the door, put the key in her pocket, and went off to bed—leaving the supper as before.

When Brownie woke up and looked out of his hole, there was, as usual, no supper for him, and the cellar was close shut. He peered about, to try and find some cranny under the door to creep out at, but there was none. And he felt so hungry that he could almost have eaten the cat, who kept walking to and fro in a melancholy manner—only she was alive, and he couldn't well eat her alive: besides, he knew she was old, and had an idea she might be tough; so he merely said, politely, "How do you do, Mrs. Pussy?" to which she answered nothing—of course.

Something must be done, and luckily Brownies can do things which nobody else can do. So he thought he would change himself into a mouse, and gnaw a hole through the door. But then he suddenly remembered the cat, who, though he had decided not to eat her, might take this opportunity of eating him. So he thought it advisable to wait till she was fast asleep, which did not happen for a good while. At length, quite tired with walking about, Pussy turned round on her tail six times, curled down in a corner, and fell fast asleep.

Immediately Brownie changed himself into the smallest mouse possible; and, taking care not to make the least noise, gnawed a hole in the door, and squeezed himself through, immediately turning into his proper shape again, for fear of accidents.

The kitchen fire was at its last glimmer; but it showed a better supper than even last night, for the Cook had had friends with her—a brother and two cousins—and they had been exceedingly merry. The food they had left behind was enough for three Brownies at least, but this one managed to eat it all up. Only once, in trying to cut a great slice of beef, he let the carving-knife and fork fall with such a clatter, that Tiny the terrier, who was tied up at the foot of the stairs, began to bark furiously. However, he brought her her puppy, which had been left in a basket in a corner of the kitchen, and so succeeded in quieting her.

After that he enjoyed himself amazingly, and made more marks than ever on the white table-cloth; for he began jumping about like a pea on a trencher, in order to make his particularly large supper agree with him.

Then, in the absence of the cat, he teased the puppy for an hour or two, till hearing the clock strike five, he thought it as well to turn into a mouse again, and creep back cautiously into his cellar. He was only just in time, for Muff opened one eye, and was just going to pounce upon him, when he changed himself back into a Brownie. She was so startled that she bounded away, her tail growing into twice its natural size, and her eyes gleaming like round green globes. But Brownie only said, "Ha, ha, ho!" and walked deliberately into his hole.

When Cook came downstairs and saw that the same thing had happened again—that the supper was all eaten, and the table-cloth blacker than ever with the extraordinary footmarks, she was greatly puzzled. Who could have done it all? Not the cat, who came mewing out of the coal-cellar the minute she unlocked the door. Possibly a rat—but then would a rat have come within reach of Tiny?

"It must have been Tiny herself, or her puppy," which just came rolling out of its basket over Cook's feet. "You little wretch! You and your mother are the greatest nuisance imaginable. I'll punish you!"

And, quite forgetting that Tiny had been safely tied up all night, and that her poor little puppy was so fat and helpless it could scarcely stand on its legs, to say nothing of jumping on chairs and tables, she gave them both such a thrashing that they ran howling together out of the kitchen door, where the kind little kitchen-maid took them up in her arms.

"You ought to have beaten the Brownie, if you could catch him," said she, in a whisper. "He will do it again and again, you'll see, for he can't bear an untidy kitchen. You'd better do as poor old Cook did, and clear the supper things away, and put the odds and ends safe in the larder; also," she added, mysteriously, "if I were you, I'd put a bowl of milk behind the coal-cellar door."

"Nonsense!" answered the young Cook, and flounced away. But afterward she thought better of it, and did as she was advised, grumbling all the time, but doing it.

Next morning the milk was gone! Perhaps Brownie had drunk it up, anyhow nobody could say that he hadn't. As for the supper, Cook having safely laid it on the shelves of the larder, nobody touched it. And the table-cloth, which was wrapped up tidily and put in the dresser drawer, came out as clean as ever, with not a single black footmark upon it. No mischief being done, the cat and the dog both escaped beating, and Brownie played no more tricks with any body—till the next time.

Adventure the Second
Brownie and the Cherry-Tree

The "next time" was quick in coming, which was not wonderful, considering there was a Brownie in the house. Otherwise the house was like most other houses, and the family like most other families. The children also: they were sometimes good, sometimes naughty, like other children; but, on the whole, they deserved to have the pleasure of a Brownie to play with them, as they declared he did— many and many a time.

A favorite play-place was the orchard, where grew the biggest cherry-tree you ever saw. They called it their "castle," because it rose up ten feet from the ground in one thick stem, and then branched out into a circle of boughs, with a flat place in the middle, where two or three children could sit at once. There they often did sit, turn by turn, or one at a time— sometimes with a book, reading; and the biggest boy made a sort of rope-ladder by which they could climb up and down— which they did all winter, and enjoyed their "castle" very much.

But one day in spring they found their ladder cut away! The Gardener had done it, saying it injured the tree, which was just coming into blossom. Now this Gardener was a rather gruff man, with a growling voice. He did not mean to be unkind, but he disliked children; he said they bothered him. But when they complained to their mother about the ladder, she agreed with Gardener that the tree must not be injured, as it bore the biggest cherries in all the neighborhood—so big that the old saying of "taking two bites at a cherry," came really true.

"Wait till the cherries are ripe," said she; and so the little people waited, and watched it through its leafing and blossoming—such sheets of blossom, white as snow!—till the fruit began to show, and grew large and red on every bough.

At last one morning the mother said, "Children, should you like to help gather the cherries to-day?"

"Hurrah!" they cried, "and not a day too soon; for we saw a flock of starlings in the next field—and if we don't clear the tree, they will."

"Very well; clear it, then. Only mind and fill my basket quite full, for preserving. What is over you may eat, if you like."

"Thank you, thank you!" and the children were eager to be off; but the mother stopped them till she could get the Gardener and his ladder.

"For it is he must climb the tree, not you; and you must do exactly as he tells you; and he will stop with you all the time and see that you don't come to harm."

This was no slight cloud on the children's happiness, and they begged hard to go alone.

"Please, might we? We will be so good!"

The mother shook her head. All the goodness in the world would not help them if they tumbled off the tree, or ate themselves sick with cherries. "You would not be safe, and I should be so unhappy!"

To make mother "unhappy" was the worst rebuke possible to these children; so they choked down their disappointment, and followed the Gardener as he walked on ahead, carrying his ladder on his shoulder. He looked very cross, and as if he did not like the children's company at all.

They were pretty good, on the whole, though they chattered a good deal; but Gardener said not a word to them all the way to the orchard. When they reached it, he just told

them to "keep out of his way and not worrit him," which they politely promised, saying among themselves that they should not enjoy their cherry-gathering at all. But children who make the best of things, and try to be as good as they can, sometimes have fun unawares.

When the Gardener was steadying his ladder against the trunk of the cherry-tree, there was suddenly heard the barking of a dog, and a very fierce dog, too. First it seemed close beside them, then in the flower-garden, then in the fowl-yard.

Gardener dropped the ladder out of his hands. "It's that Boxer! He has got loose again! He will be running after my chickens, and dragging his broken chain all over my borders. And he is so fierce, and so delighted to get free. He'll bite any body who ties him up, except me."

"Hadn't you better you go and see after him?"

Gardener thought it was the eldest boy who spoke, and turned round angrily; but the little fellow had never opened his lips.

Here there was heard a still louder bark, and from a quite different part of the garden.

"There he is—I'm sure of it! jumping over my bedding-out plants, and breaking my cucumber frames. Abominable beast!—just let me catch him!" Off Gardener darted in a violent passion, throwing the ladder down upon the grass, and forgetting all about the cherries and the children.

The instant he was gone, a shrill laugh, loud and merry, was heard close by, and a little brown old man's face peeped from behind the cherry-tree.

"How d'ye do?—Boxer was me. Didn't I bark well? Now I'm come to play with you."

The children clapped their hands; for they knew they were going to have some fun if Brownie was there—he was the best little playfellow in the world. And then they had him all to themselves. Nobody ever saw him except the children.

"Come on!" cried he, in his shrill voice, half like an old man's, half like a baby's. "Who'll begin to gather the cherries?"

They all looked blank; for the tree was so high to where the branches sprang, and besides, their mother had said they were not to climb. And the ladder lay flat upon the grass—far too heavy for little hands to move.

"What! you big boys don't expect a poor little fellow like me to lift the ladder all by myself? Try! I'll help you."

Whether he helped or not, no sooner had they taken hold of the ladder than it rose up, almost of its own accord, and fixed itself quite safely against the tree.

"But we must not climb—mother told us not," said the boys, ruefully. "Mother said we were to stand at the bottom and pick up the cherries."

"Very well. Obey your mother. I'll just run up the tree myself."

Before the words were out of his mouth Brownie darted up the ladder like a monkey, and disappeared among the fruit-laden branches.

The children looked dismayed for a minute, till they saw a merry brown face peeping out from the green leaves at the very top of the tree.

"Biggest fruit always grows highest," cried the Brownie. "Stand in a row, all you children. Little boys, hold out your caps: little girls, make a bag of your pinafores. Open your mouths and shut your eyes, and see what the queen will send you."

They laughed and did as they were told; whereupon they were drowned in a shower of cherries—cherries falling like hailstones, hitting them on their heads, their cheeks, their noses—filling their caps and pinafores, and then rolling and tumbling on to the grass, till it was strewn thick as leaves in autumn with the rosy fruit.

What a glorious scramble they had—these three little boys and three little girls! How they laughed and jumped and knocked their heads together in picking up the cherries, yet never quarreled—for there were such heaps, it would have been ridiculous to squabble over them; and besides, whenever they began to quarrel, Brownie always ran away. Now he was the merriest of the lot; ran up and down the tree like a cat, helped to pick up the cherries, and was first-rate at filling the large market-basket.

"We were to eat as many as we liked, only we must first fill the basket," conscientiously said the eldest girl; upon which they all set to at once, and filled it to the brim.

"Now we'll have a dinner-party," cried the Brownie; and squatted down like a Turk, crossed his queer little legs, and sticking his elbows upon his knees, in a way that nobody but a Brownie could manage. "Sit in a ring! sit in a ring! and we'll see who can eat fastest."

The children obeyed. How many cherries they devoured, and how fast they did it, passes my capacity of telling. I only hope they were not ill next day, and that all the cherry-stones they swallowed by mistake did not disagree with them. But perhaps nothing does disagree with one when one dines with a Brownie. They ate so much, laughing in equal proportion, that they had quite forgotten the Gardener—when, all of a sudden, they heard him clicking angrily the orchard gate, and talking to himself as he walked through.

"That nasty dog! It wasn't Boxer, after all. A nice joke! to find him quietly asleep in his kennel after having hunted him, as I thought, from one end of the garden to the other! Now for the cherries and the children—bless us, where are the children?

And the cherries? Why, the tree is as bare as a blackthorn in February! The starlings have been at it, after all. Oh dear! oh dear!"

"Oh dear! oh dear!" echoed a voice from behind the tree, followed by shouts of mocking laughter. Not from the children—they sat as demure as possible, all in a ring, with their hands before them, and in the centre the huge basket of cherries, piled as full as it could possibly hold. But the Brownie had disappeared.

"You naughty brats, I'll have you punished!" cried the Gardener, furious at the laughter, for he never laughed himself. But as there was nothing wrong; the cherries being gathered—a very large crop—and the ladder found safe in its place—it was difficult to say what had been the harm done and who had done it.

So he went growling back to the house, carrying the cherries to the mistress, who coaxed him into good temper again, as she sometimes did; bidding also the children to behave well to him, since he was an old man, and not really bad—only cross. As for the little folks, she had not the slightest intention of punishing them; and, as for Brownie, it was impossible to catch him. So nobody was punished at all.

Adventure the Third
Brownie in the Farmyard

Which was a place where he did not often go, for he preferred being warm and snug in the house. But when he felt himself ill-used, he would wander anywhere, in order to play tricks upon those whom he thought had done him harm; for, being only a Brownie, and not a man, he did not understand that the best way to revenge yourself upon your enemies is either to let them alone or to pay them back good for evil—it disappoints them so much, and makes them so exceedingly ashamed of themselves.

One day Brownie overheard the Gardener advising the Cook to put sour milk into his bowl at night, instead of sweet.

"He'd never find out the difference, no more than the pigs do. Indeed, it's my belief that a pig, or dog, or something, empties the bowl, and not a Brownie, at all. It's just clean waste—that's what I say."

"Then you'd better hold your tongue, and mind your own business," returned the Cook, who was of a sharp temper, and would not stand being meddled with. She began to abuse the Gardener soundly; but his wife, who was standing by, took his part, as she always did when any third party scolded him. So they all squabbled together, till Brownie, hid under his coal, put his little hands over his little ears.

"Dear me, what a noise these mortals do make when they quarrel! They quite deafen me. I must teach them better manners."

But when the Cook slammed the door to, and left Gardener and his wife alone, they too began to dispute between themselves.

"You make such a fuss over your nasty pigs, and get all the scraps for them," said the wife. "It's of much more importance that I should have everything Cook can spare for my chickens. Never were such fine chickens as my last brood!"

"I thought they were ducklings."

"How you catch me up, you rude old man! They are ducklings, and beauties, too—even though they have never seen water. Where's the pond you promised to make for me, I wonder?"

"Rubbish, woman! If my cows do without a pond, your ducklings may. And why will you be so silly as to rear ducklings at all? Fine fat chickens are a deal better. You'll find out your mistake some day."

"And so will you when that old Alderney runs dry. You'll wish you had taken my advice, and fattened and sold her."

"Alderney cows won't sell for fattening, and women's advice is never worth twopence. Yours isn't worth even a half-penny. What are you laughing at?"

"I wasn't laughing," said the wife, angrily; and, in truth, it was not she, but little Brownie, running under the barrow which the Gardener was wheeling along, and very much amused that people should be so silly as to squabble about nothing.

It was still early morning; for, whatever this old couple's faults might be, laziness was not one of them. The wife rose with the dawn to feed her poultry and collect her eggs; the husband also got through as much work by breakfast-time as many an idle man does by noon. But Brownie had been beforehand with them this day.

When all the fowls came running to be fed, the big Brahma hen who had watched the ducklings was seen wandering forlornly about, and clucking mournfully for her young brood— she could not find them anywhere. Had she been able to speak, she might have told how a large white Aylesbury duck had waddled into the farmyard, and waddled out again, coaxing them after her, no doubt in search of a pond. But missing they were, most certainly.

"Cluck, cluck, cluck!" mourned the miserable hen-mother—and, "Oh, my ducklings, my ducklings!" cried the Gardener's wife—"Who can have carried off my beautiful ducklings?"

"Rats, maybe," said the Gardener, cruelly, as he walked away. And as he went he heard the squeak of a rat below his wheelbarrow. But he could not catch it, any more than his wife could catch the Aylesbury duck. Of course not. Both were—the Brownie!

Just at this moment the six little people came running into the farmyard. When they had been particularly good, they were sometimes allowed to go with Gardener a-milking, each carrying his or her own mug for a drink of milk, warm from the cow. They scampered after him—a noisy tribe, begging to be taken down to the field, and holding out their six mugs entreatingly.

"What! six cupfuls of milk, when I haven't a drop to spare, and Cook is always wanting more? Ridiculous nonsense! Get along with you; you may come to the field—I can't hinder that—but you'll get no milk to-day. Take your mugs back again to the kitchen."

The poor little folks made the best of a bad business, and obeyed; then followed Gardener down to the field, rather dolefully. But it was such a beautiful morning that they soon recovered their spirits. The grass shone with dew, like a sheet of diamonds, the clover smelled so sweet, and two skylarks were singing at one another high up in the sky. Several rabbits darted past, to their great amusement, especially one very large

rabbit—brown, not gray—which dodged them in and out, and once nearly threw Gardener down, pail and all, by running across his feet; which set them all laughing, till they came where Dolly, the cow, lay chewing the cud under a large oak-tree.

It was great fun to stir her up, as usual, and lie down, one after the other, in the place where she had lain all night long, making the grass flat, and warm, and perfumy with her sweet breath. She let them do it, and then stood meekly by; for Dolly was the gentlest cow in the world.

But this morning something strange seemed to possess her. She altogether refused to be milked—kicked, plunged, tossed over the pail, which was luckily empty.

"Bless the cow! what's wrong with her? It's surely you children's fault. Stand off, the whole lot of you. Soh, Dolly! good Dolly!"

But Dolly was any thing but good. She stood switching her tail, and looking as savage as so mild an animal possibly could look.

"It's all your doing, you naughty children! You have been playing her some trick, I know," cried the Gardener, in great wrath.

They assured him they had done nothing, and indeed, they looked as quiet as mice and as innocent as lambs. At length the biggest boy pointed out a large wasp which had settled in Dolly's ear.

"That accounts for everything," said the Gardener.

But it did not mend everything; for when he tried to drive it away it kept coming back and back again, and buzzing round his own head and the cow's with a voice that the children thought was less like a buzz of a wasp than the sound of a person laughing. At length it frightened Dolly to such an extent that, with one wild bound she darted right away, and galloped off to the farther end of the field.

"I'll get a rope and tie her legs together," cried the Gardener, fiercely. "She shall repent giving me all this trouble—that she shall!"

"Ha, ha, ha!" laughed somebody. The Gardener thought it was the children, and gave one of them an angry cuff as he walked away. But they knew it was somebody else, and were not at all surprised when, the minute his back was turned, Dolly came walking quietly back, led by a little wee brown man who scarcely reached up to her knees. Yet she let him guide her, which he did as gently as possible, though the string he held her by was no thicker than a spider web, floating from one of her horns.

"Soh, Dolly! good Dolly!" cried Brownie, mimicking the Gardener's voice. "Now we'll see what we can do. I want my breakfast badly—don't you, little folks?"

Of course they did, for the morning air made them very hungry.

"Very well—wait a bit, though. Old people should be served first, you know. Besides, I want to go to bed."

"Go to bed in the daylight!" The children all laughed, and then looked quite shy and sorry, lest they might have seemed rude to the little Brownie. But he—he liked fun; and never took offence when none was meant.

He placed himself on the milking-stool, which was so high that his little legs were dangling half-way down, and milked and milked—Dolly standing as still as possible—till he had filled the whole pail. Most astonishing cow! she gave as much as two cows; and such delicious milk as it was—all frothing and yellow—richer than even Dolly's milk had ever been before. The children's mouths watered for it, but not a word said they—even when, instead of giving it to them, Brownie put his own mouth to the pail, and drank and drank, till it seemed as if he were never going to stop. But it was decidedly a relief to them when he popped his head up again, and lo! the pail was as full as ever!

"Now, little ones, now's your turn. Where are your mugs?"

All answered mournfully, "We've got none. Gardener made us take them back again."

"Never mind—all right. Gather me half a dozen of the biggest buttercups you can find."

"What nonsense!" thought the children; but they did it. Brownie laid the flowers in a row upon the eldest girl's lap—blew upon them one by one, and each turned into the most beautiful golden cup that ever was seen!

~ 19 ~

"Now, then, every one take his own mug, and I'll fill it."

He milked away—each child got a drink, and then the cups were filled again. And all the while Dolly stood as quiet as possible—looking benignly round, as if she would be happy to supply milk to the whole parish, if the Brownie desired it.

"Soh, Dolly! Thank you, Dolly!" said he, again, mimicking the Gardener's voice, half growling, half coaxing. And while he spoke, the real voice was heard behind the hedge. There was a sound as of a great wasp flying away, which made Dolly prick up her ears, and look as if the old savageness was coming back upon her. The children snatched up their mugs, but there was no need, they had all turned into buttercups again.

Gardener jumped over the stile, as cross as two sticks, with an old rope in his hand.

"Oh, what a bother I've had! Breakfast ready, and no milk yet—and such a row as they are making over those lost ducklings. Stand back, you children, and don't hinder me a minute. No use begging—not a drop of milk shall you get. Hillo, Dolly? Quiet old girl!"

Quiet enough she was this time—but you might as well have milked a plaster cow in a London milking-shop. Not one ringing drop resounded against the empty pail; for, when they peeped in, the children saw, to their amazement, that it was empty.

"The creature's bewitched!" cried the Gardener, in a great fury. "Or else somebody has milked her dry already. Have you done it? or you?" he asked each of the children.

They might have said No—which was the literal truth—but then it would not have been the whole truth, for they knew quite well that Dolly had been milked, and also who had done it. And their mother had always taught them that to make a person believe a lie is nearly as bad as telling him one. Yet still they did not like to betray the kind little Brownie. Greatly puzzled, they hung their heads and said nothing.

"Look in your pail again," cried a voice from the other side of Dolly. And there at the bottom was just the usual quantity of milk—no more and no less.

The Gardener was very much astonished. "It must be the Brownie!" muttered he, in a frightened tone; and, taking off his hat, "Thank you, sir," said he to Mr. Nobody—at which the children all burst out laughing. But they kept their own counsel, and he was afraid to ask them any more questions.

By-and-by his fright wore off a little. "I only hope the milk is good milk, and will poison nobody," said he, sulkily. "However, that's not my affair. You children had better tell your mother all about it. I left her in the farmyard in a pretty state of mind about her ducklings."

Perhaps Brownie heard this, and was sorry, for he liked the children's mother, who had always been kind to him. Besides, he never did any body harm who did not deserve it; and though, being a Brownie, he could hardly be said to have a conscience, he had something which stood in the place of one—a liking to see people happy rather than miserable.

So, instead of going to bed under his big coal for the day, when, after breakfast, the children and their mother came out to look at a new brood of chickens, he crept after them and hid behind the hencoop where the old mother-hen was put, with her young ones round her.

There had been great difficulty in getting her in there, for she was a hen who hatched her brood on independent principles. Instead of sitting upon the nice nest that the Gardener made for her, she had twice gone into a little wood close by and made a nest for herself, which nobody could ever find; and where she hatched in secret, coming every second day to be fed, and then vanishing again, till at last she re-appeared in triumph, with her chickens running after her. The first brood there had been twelve, but of this there were fourteen—all from her own eggs, of course, and she was uncommonly proud of them. So was the Gardener, so was the mistress—who liked all young things. Such a picture as they were! fourteen soft, yellow, fluffy things, running about after their mother. It had been a most troublesome business to catch—first her, and then them, to put them under the coop. The old hen resisted, and pecked furiously at Gardener's legs, and the chickens ran about in frantic terror, chirping wildly in answer to her clucking.

At last, however, the little family was safe in shelter, and the chickens counted over, to see that none had been lost in the scuffle. How funny they were! looking so innocent and yet so wise, as chickens do—peering out at the world from under their mother's wing, or hopping over her back, or snuggled all together under her breast, so that nothing was seen of them but a mass of yellow legs, like a great centiped.

"How happy the old hen is," said the children's mother, looking on, and then looking compassionately at that other forlorn old hen, who had hatched the ducklings, and kept wandering about the farmyard, clucking miserably, "Those poor ducklings, what can have become of them? If rats had killed them, we should have found feathers or something; and weasels would have sucked their brains and left them. They must have been stolen, or wandered away, and died of cold and hunger—my poor ducklings!"

The mistress sighed, for she could not bear any living thing to suffer. And the children nearly cried at the thought of what might be happening to their pretty ducklings. That very minute a little wee brown face peered through a hole in the hencoop, making the old mother-hen fly furiously at it—as she did at the slightest shadow of an enemy to her little ones. However, no harm happened—only a guinea-fowl suddenly ran across the farmyard, screaming in its usual harsh voice. But it was not the usual sort of guinea-fowl, being larger and handsomer than any of theirs.

"Oh, what a beauty of a creature! how did it ever come into our farmyard," cried the delighted children; and started off after it, to catch it if possible.

But they ran, and they ran—through the gate and out into the lane; and the guinea-fowl still ran on before them, until, turning round a corner, they lost sight of it, and immediately saw something else, equally curious. Sitting on the top of a big thistle—so big that he must have had to climb it just like a tree—was the Brownie. His legs were crossed, and his arms too, his little brown cap was stuck knowingly on one side, and he was laughing heartily.

"How do you do? Here I am again. I thought I wouldn't go to bed after all. Shall I help you to find the ducklings? Very well! come along."

They crossed the field, Brownie running beside them, and as fast as they could, though he looked such an old man; and sometimes turning over on legs and arms like a Catherine wheel—which they tried to imitate, but generally failed, and only bruised their fingers and noses.

He lured them on and on till they came to the wood, and to a green path in it, which well as they knew the neighborhood, none of the children had ever seen before. It led to a most beautiful pond, as clear as crystal and as blue as the sky. Large trees grew round it, dipping their branches in the water, as if they were looking at themselves in a glass. And all about their roots were quantities of primroses—the biggest primroses the little girls had ever seen. Down they dropped on their fat knees, squashing more primroses than they gathered, though they tried to gather them all; and the smallest child even began to cry because her hands were so full that the flowers dropped through her fingers. But the boys, older and more practical, rather despised primroses.

"I thought we had come to look for ducklings," said the eldest. "Mother is fretting dreadfully about her ducklings. Where can they be?"

"Shut your eyes, and you'll see," said the Brownie, at which they all laughed, but did it; and when they opened their eyes again, what should they behold but a whole fleet of ducklings sailing out from the roots of an old willow-tree, one after the other, looking as fat and content as possible, and swimming as naturally as if they had lived on a pond—and this particularly pond, all their days.

"Count them," said the Brownie, "the whole eight—quite correct. And then try and catch them—if you can."

Easier said than done. The boys set to work with great satisfaction—boys do so enjoy hunting something. They coaxed them—they shouted at them—they threw little sticks at them; but as soon as they wanted them to go one way the fleet of ducklings immediately turned round and sailed another way, doing it so deliberately and majestically, that the children could not help laughing. As for little Brownie, he sat on a branch of the willow-tree, with his legs dangling down to the surface of the pond, kicking at the water-spiders, and grinning with all his might. At length, quite tired out, in spite of their fun, the children begged for his help, and he took compassion on them.

"Turn round three times and see what you can find," shouted he.

Immediately each little boy found in his arms, and each little girl in her pinafore, a fine fat duckling. And there being eight of them, the two elder children had each a couple. They were rather cold and damp, and slightly uncomfortable to cuddle, ducks not being used to cuddling. Poor things! they struggled hard to get away. But the children hugged them tight, and ran as fast as their legs could carry them through the wood, forgetting, in their joy, even to say "Thank you" to the little Brownie.

When they reached their mother she was as glad as they, for she never thought to see her ducklings again; and to have them back alive and uninjured, and watch them running to the old hen, who received them with an ecstasy of delight, was so exciting, that nobody thought of asking a single question as to where they had been found.

When the mother did ask, the children told her about Brownie's taking them to the beautiful pond—and what a wonderful pond it was; how green the trees were round it; and how large the primroses grew. They never tired of talking about it and seeking for it. But the odd thing was that, seek as they might, they never could find it again. Many a day did the little people roam about one by one, or all together, round the wood, often getting themselves sadly draggled with mud and torn with brambles—but the beautiful pond they never found again.

Nor did the ducklings, I suppose; for they wandered no more from the farmyard, to the old mother-hen's great content. They grew up into fat and respectable ducks—five white ones and three gray ones—waddling about, very content, though they never saw water, except the tank which was placed for them to paddle in. They lived a lazy, peaceful, pleasant life for a long time, and were at last killed and eaten with green peas, one after the other, to the family's great satisfaction, if not to their own.

Adventure the Fourth
Brownie's Ride

For the little Brownie, though not given to horsemanship, did once take a ride, and a very remarkable one it was. Shall I tell you all about it?

The six little children got a present of something they had longed for all their lives—a pony. Not a rocking-horse, but a real live pony—a Shetland pony, too, which had traveled all the way from the Shetland Isles to Devonshire—where every body wondered at it, for such a creature had not been seen in the neighborhood for years and years. She was no bigger than a donkey, and her coat, instead of being smooth like a horse's, was shaggy like a young bear's. She had a long tail, which had never been cut, and such a deal of hair in her mane and over her eyes that it gave her quite a fierce countenance. In fact, among the mild and tame Devonshire beasts, the little Shetland pony looked almost like a wild animal. But in reality she was the gentlest creature in the world. Before she had been many days with them, she began to know the children quite well; followed them about, ate corn out of the bowl they held out to her; nay, one day, when the eldest little girl offered her bread-and-butter, she stooped her head and took it from the child's hand, just like a young lady. Indeed, Jess—that was her name—was altogether so lady-like in her behavior, that more than once Cook allowed her to walk in at the back-door, when she stood politely warming her nose at the kitchen-fire for a minute or two, then turned round and as politely walked out again. But she never did any mischief; and was so quiet and gentle a creature that she bade fair soon to become as great a pet in the household as the dog, the cat, the kittens, the puppies, the fowls, the ducks, the cow, the pig, and all the other members of the family.

The only one who disliked her, and grumbled at her, was the Gardener. This was odd; because, though cross to children, the old man was kind to dumb beasts. Even his pig knew his voice and grunted, and held out his nose to be scratched; and he always gave each successive pig a name, Jack or Dick, and called them by it, and was quite affectionate to them, one after the other, until the very day that they were killed. But they were English pigs—and the pony was Scotch—and the Devonshire Gardener hated every thing Scotch, he said; besides, he was not used to groom's work, and the pony required such a deal of grooming on account of her long hair. More than once Gardener threatened to clip it short, and turn her into a regular English pony, but the children were in such distress and mother forbade any such spoiling of Jessie's personal appearance.

At length, to keep things smooth, and to avoid the rough words and even blows which poor Jess sometimes got, they sought in the village for a boy to look after her, and found a great rough, shock-headed lad named Bill, who, for a few shillings a week, consented to come up every morning and learn the beginning of a groom's business; hoping to end, as his mother said he should, in sitting, like the squire's fat coachman, as broad as he was long, on the top of the hammer-cloth of a grand carriage, and do nothing all day but drive a pair of horses as stout as himself a few miles along the road and back again.

Bill would have liked this very much, he thought, if he could have been a coachman all at once, for if there was one thing he disliked, it was work. He much preferred to lie in the sun all day and do nothing; and he only agreed to come and take care of Jess because she was such a very little pony, that looking after her seemed next door to doing nothing. But when he tried it, he found his mistake. True, Jess was a very gentle beast, so quiet that the old mother-hen with fourteen chicks used, instead of roosting with the rest of the fowls, to come regularly into the portion of the cow-shed which was partitioned off for a stable, and settle under a corner of Jess's manger for the night; and in the morning the chicks would be seen running about fearlessly among her feet and under her very nose.

But, for all that, she required a little management, for she did not like her long hair to be roughly handled; it took a long time to clean her; and, though she did not scream out like some silly little children when her hair was combed, I am afraid she sometimes kicked and bounced about, giving Bill a deal of trouble—all the more trouble, the more impatient Bill was.

And then he had to keep within call, for the children wanted their pony at all hours. She was their own especial property, and they insisted upon learning to ride—even before they got a saddle. Hard work it was to stick on Jess's bare back, but by degrees the boys did it, turn and turn about, and even gave their sisters a turn too—a very little one—just once round the field and back again, which was quite enough, they considered, for girls. But they were very kind to their little sisters, held them on so that they could not fall, and led Jess carefully and quietly: and altogether behaved as elder brothers should.

Nor did they squabble very much among themselves, though sometimes it was rather difficult to keep their turns all fair, and remember accurately which was which. But they did their best, being, on the whole, extremely good children. And they were so happy to have their pony, that they would have been ashamed to quarrel over her.

Also, one very curious thing kept them on their good behavior. Whenever they did begin to misconduct themselves—to want to ride out of their turns, or to domineer over one another, or the boys, joining together, tried to domineer over the girls, as I grieve to say boys not seldom do—they used to hear in the air, right over their heads, the crack of an unseen whip. It was none of theirs, for they had not got a whip; that was a felicity which their father had promised when they could all ride like a young gentleman and ladies; but there was no mistaking the sound—indeed, it always startled Jess so that she set off galloping, and could not be caught again for many minutes.

This happened several times, until one of them said, "Perhaps it's the Brownie." Whether it was or not, it made them behave better for a good while; till one unfortunate day the two eldest began contending which should ride foremost and which hindmost on Jess's back, when "Crick—crack!" went the whip in the air, frightening the pony so much that she kicked up her heels, tossed both the boys over her head, and scampered off, followed by a loud "Ha, ha, ha!"

It certainly did not come from the two boys, who had fallen—quite safely, but rather unpleasantly—into a large nettle-bed; whence they crawled out, rubbing their arms and legs, and looking too much ashamed to complain. But they were rather frightened and a little cross, for Jess took a skittish fit, and refused to be caught and mounted again, till the bell rang for school—when she grew as meek as possible. Too late—for the children were obliged to run indoors, and got no more rides for the whole day.

Jess was from this incident supposed to be on the same friendly terms with Brownie as were the rest of the household. Indeed, when she came, the children had taken care to lead her up to the coal-cellar door and introduce her properly—for they knew Brownie was very jealous of strangers, and often played them tricks. But after that piece of civility he would be sure, they thought, to take her under his protection. And sometimes, when the little Shetlander was restless and pricked up her ears, looking preternaturally wise under those shaggy brows of hers, the children used to say to one another, "Perhaps she sees the Brownie."

Whether she did or not, Jess sometimes seemed to see a good deal that others did not see, and was apparently a favorite with the Brownie, for she grew and thrived so much that she soon became the pride and delight of the children and of the whole family. You would hardly have known her for the rough, shaggy, half-starved little beast that had arrived a few weeks before. Her coat was so silky, her limbs so graceful, and her head so full of intelligence, that every body admired her. Then even Gardener began to admire her too.

"I think I'll get upon her back; it will save me walking down to the village," said he, one day. And she actually carried him—though, as his feet nearly touched the ground, it looked as if the man were carrying the pony, and not the pony the man.

And the children laughed so immoderately, that he never tried it afterward.

Nor Bill neither, though he had once thought he should like a ride, and got astride on Jess; but she quickly ducked her head down, and he tumbled over it. Evidently she had her own tastes as to her riders, and much preferred little people to big ones.

Pretty Jess! when cantering round the paddock with the young folk she really was quite a picture. And when at last she got a saddle—a new, beautiful saddle, with a pommel to take off and on, so as to suit both boys and girls—how proud they all were, Jess included! That day they were allowed to take her into the market-town—Gardener leading her, as Bill could not be trusted—and every body, even the blacksmith, who hoped by-and-by to have the pleasure of shoeing her, said, what a beautiful pony she was!

After this, Gardener treated Jess a great deal better, and showed Bill how to groom her, and kept him close at it too, which Bill did not like at all. He was a very lazy lad, and whenever he could shirk work he did it; and many a time when the children wanted Jess, either there was nobody to saddle her, or she had not been properly groomed, or Bill was away at his dinner, and they had to wait till he came back and could put her in order to be taken out for a ride like a genteel animal—which I am afraid neither pony nor children enjoyed half so much as the old ways before Bill came.

Still, they were gradually becoming excellent little horsemen and horsewomen—even the youngest, only four years old, whom all the rest were very tender over, and who was often

~ 30 ~

held on Jess's back and given a ride out of her turn because she was a good little girl, and never cried for it. And seldomer and seldomer was heard the mysterious sound of the whip in the air, which warned them of quarreling—Brownie hated quarreling.

In fact, their only trouble was Bill, who never came to his work in time, and never did things when wanted, and was ill-natured, lazy, and cross to the children, so that they disliked him very much.

"I wish the Brownie would punish you," said one of the boys; "you'd behave better then."

"The Brownie!" cried Bill, contemptuously; "if I caught him, I'd kick him up in the air like this!"

And he kicked up his cap—his only cap, it was—which, strange to relate, flew right up, ever so high, and lodged at the very top of a tree which overhung the stable, where it dangled for weeks and weeks, during which time poor Bill had to go bareheaded.

He was very much vexed, and revenged himself by vexing the children in all sorts of ways. They would have told their mother, and asked her to send Bill away, only she had a great many anxieties just then, for their old grandmother was very ill, and they did not like to make a fuss about any thing that would trouble her.

So Bill staid on, and nobody found out what a bad, ill-natured, lazy boy he was.

But one day the mother was sent for suddenly, not knowing when she should be able to come home again. She was very sad, and so were the children, for they loved their grandmother—and as the carriage drove off they all stood crying round the front-door for ever so long.

The servants even cried too—all but Bill.

"It's an ill wind that blows nobody good," said he. "What a jolly time I shall have! I'll do nothing all day long. Those troublesome children sha'n't have Jess to ride; I'll keep her in the stable, and then she won't get dirty, and I shall have no trouble in cleaning her. Hurrah! what fun!"

He put his hands in his pockets, and sat whistling the best part of the afternoon.

The children had been so unhappy, that for that day they quite forgot Jess; but next morning, after lessons were over, they came begging for a ride.

"You can't get one. The stable-door's locked and I've lost the key." (He had it in his pocket all the time.)

"How is poor Jess to get her dinner?" cried a thoughtful little girl. "Oh, how hungry she will be!"

And the child was quite in distress, as were the two other girls. But the boys were more angry than sorry.

"It was very stupid of you, Bill, to lose the key. Look about and find it, or else break open the door."

"I won't," said Bill; "I dare say the key will turn up before night, and if it doesn't, who cares? You get riding enough and too much. I'll not bother myself about it, or Jess either."

And Bill sauntered away. He was a big fellow, and the little lads were rather afraid of him. But as he walked, he could not keep his hand out of his trowsers-pocket, where the key felt growing heavier and heavier, till he expected it every minute to tumble through and come out at his boots—convicting him before all the children of having told a lie.

Nobody was in the habit of telling lies to them, so they never suspected him, but went innocently searching about for the key—Bill all the while clutching it fast. But every time he touched it, he felt his fingers pinched, as if there was a cockroach in his pocket—or little lobster—or something, anyhow, that had claws. At last, fairly frightened, he made an excuse to go into the cow-shed, took the key out of his pocket and looked at it, and finally hid it in a corner of the manger, among the hay.

As he did so, he heard a most extraordinary laugh, which was certainly not from Dolly the cow, and, as he went out of the shed, he felt the same sort of pinch at his ankles, which made him so angry that he kept striking with his whip in all directions, but hit nobody for nobody was there.

But Jess—who, as soon as she heard the children's voices, set up a most melancholy whinnying behind the locked stable-door—began to neigh energetically. And Boxer barked, and the hens cackled, and the guinea-fowls cried "Come back, come back!" in their usual insane fashion—indeed, the whole

~ 32 ~

farmyard seemed in such an excited state, that the children got frightened lest Gardener should scold them, and ran away, leaving Bill master of the field.

What an idle day he had! How he sat on the wall with his hands in his pockets, and lounged upon the fence, and sauntered around the garden! At length, absolutely tired of doing nothing, he went and talked with the Gardener's wife while she was hanging out her clothes. Gardener had gone down to the lower field, with all the little folks after him, so that he knew nothing of Bill's idling, or it might have come to an end.

By-and-by Bill thought it was time to go home to his supper. "But first I'll give Jess her corn," said he, "double quantity, and then I need not come back to give her her breakfast so early in the morning. Soh! you greedy beast! I'll be at you presently, if you don't stop that noise."

For Jess, at sound of his footsteps, was heard to whinny in the most imploring manner, enough to have melted a heart of stone.

"The key—where on earth did I put the key?" cried Bill, whose constant habit it was to lay things out of his hand and then forget where he had put them, causing himself endless loss of time in searching for them—as now. At last he suddenly remembered the corner of the cow's manger, where he felt sure he had left it. But the key was not there.

"You can't have eaten it, you silly old cow," said he, striking Dolly on the nose as she rubbed herself against him— she was an affectionate beast. "Nor you, you stupid old hen!" kicking the mother of the brood, who, with her fourteen chicks, being shut out of their usual roosting-place—Jess's stable—kept pecking about under Dolly's legs. "It can't have gone without hands—of course it can't." But most certainly the key was gone.

What in the world should Bill do? Jess kept on making a pitiful complaining. No wonder, as she had not tasted food since morning. It would have made any kind-hearted person quite sad to hear her, thinking how exceedingly hungry the poor pony must be.

Little did Bill care for that, or for anything, except that he should be sure to get into trouble as soon as he was found out. When he heard Gardener coming into the farmyard, with the children after him, Bill bolted over the wall like a flash of lightning, and ran away home, leaving poor Jess to her fate.

All the way he seemed to hear at his heels a little dog yelping, and then a swarm of gnats buzzing round his head, and altogether was so perplexed and bewildered, that when he got into his mother's cottage he escaped into bed, and pulled the blanket over his ears to shut out the noise of the dog and the gnats, which at last turned into a sound like somebody laughing. It was not his mother, she didn't often laugh, poor soul!—Bill bothered her quite too much for that, and he knew it. Dreadfully frightened, he hid his head under the bedclothes, determined to go to sleep and think about nothing till next day.

Meantime Gardener returned, with all the little people trooping after him. He had been rather kinder to them than usual this day, because he knew their mother had gone away in trouble, and now he let them help him to roll the gravel, and fetch up Dolly to be milked, and watch him milk her in the cow-shed—where, it being nearly winter, she always spent the night now. They were so well amused that they forgot all about their disappointment as to the ride, and Jess did not remind them of it by her whinnying. For as soon as Bill was gone she grew silent.

At last one little girl, the one who had cried over Jess's being left hungry, remembered the poor pony, and, peeping through a crevice in the cow-shed, saw her stand contentedly munching at a large bowlful of corn.

"So Bill did find the key. I'm very glad," thought the kind little maiden, and to make sure looked again, when—what do you think she beheld squatting on the manger? Something brown—either a large brown rat, or a small brown man. But she held her tongue, since, being a very little girl, people sometimes laughed at her for the strange things she saw. She was quite certain she did see them, for all that.

So she and the rest of the children went indoors and to bed. When they were fast asleep, something happened. Something so curious, that the youngest boy, who, thinking he heard Jess neighing, got up to look out, was afraid to tell, lest he too should be laughed at, and went back to bed immediately.

In the middle of the night, a little old brown man carrying a lantern, or at least having a light in his hand that looked like a lantern—went and unlocked Jess's stable, and patted her pretty head. At first she started, but soon she grew quiet and pleased, and let him do what he chose with her. He began rubbing her down, making the same funny hissing with his mouth that Bill did, and all grooms do—I never could find out why. But Jess evidently liked it, and stood as good as possible.

"Isn't it nice to be clean?" said the wee man, talking to her as if she were a human being, or a Brownie. "And I dare say your poor little legs ache with standing so long. Shall we have a run together? the moon shines bright in the clear, cold night. Dear me! I'm talking poetry."

But Brownies are not poetical fairies, quite commonplace, and up to all sorts of work. So, while he talked, he was saddling and bridling Jess, she not objecting in the least. Finally, he jumped on her back.

"'Off, said the stranger—off, off, and away!'" sang Brownie mimicking a song of the Cook's. People in that house often heard their songs repeated in the oddest way, from room to room, everybody fancying it was somebody else that did it. But it was only the Brownie. "Now, 'A southerly wind and a cloudy sky proclaim a hunting morning!'"

Or night—for it was the middle of the night, though bright as day—and Jess galloped and the Brownie sat on her back as merrily as if they had gone hunting together all their days.

Such a steeple-chase it was! They cleared the farmyard at a single bound, and went flying down the road, and across the ploughed field, and into the wood. Then out into the open country, and by-and-by into a dark, muddy lane—and oh! how muddy Devonshire lanes can be sometimes!

"Let's go into the water to wash ourselves," said Brownie, and coaxed Jess into a deep stream, which she swam as bravely as possible—she had not had such a frolic since she left her native Shetland Isles. Up the bank she scrambled, her long hair dripping as if she had been a water-dog instead of a pony. Brownie, too, shook himself like a rat or a beaver, throwing a shower round him in all directions.

"Never mind; at it again, my lass!" and he urged Jess into the water once more. Out she came, wetter and brisker than ever, and went back home again through the lane, and the wood, and the ploughed field, galloping like the wind, and tossing back her ears and mane and tail, perfectly frantic with enjoyment.

But when she reached her stable, the plight she was in would have driven any respectable groom frantic too. Her sides were white with foam, and the mud was sticking all over her like a plaster. As for her beautiful long hair, it was all caked together in a tangle, as if all the combs in the world would never make it smooth again. Her mane especially was plaited into knots, which people in Devonshire call elf-locks, and say, when they find them on their horses, that it is because the fairies have been riding them.

Certainly, poor Jess had been pretty well ridden that night. When just as the dawn began to break, Gardener got up and looked into the farmyard, his sharp eye caught sight of the stable-door wide open.

"Well done, Bill," shouted he, "up early at last. One hour before breakfast is worth three after."

But no Bill was there; only Jess, trembling and shaking, all in a foam, and muddy from head to foot, but looking perfectly cheerful in her mind. And out from under her fore legs ran a small creature which Gardener mistook for Tiny, only Tiny was gray, and this dog was brown, of course!

I should not like to tell you all that was said to Bill when, an hour after breakfast-time, he came skulking up to the farm. In fact, words failing, Gardener took a good stick and laid it about Bill's shoulders, saying he would either do this, or tell the mistress of him, and how he had left the stable-door open all night, and some bad fellow had stolen Jess, and galloped her all across the country, till, if she hadn't been the cleverest pony in the world, she never could have got back again.

Bill durst not contradict this explanation of the story, especially as the key was found hanging up in its proper place by the kitchen door. And when he went to fetch it, he heard the most extraordinary sound in the coal-cellar close by—like somebody snoring or laughing. Bill took to his heels, and did not come back for a whole hour.

But when he did come back, he made himself as busy as possible. He cleaned Jess, which was half a day's work at least. Then he took the little people a ride, and afterward put his stable in the most beautiful order, and altogether was such a changed Bill, that Gardener told him he must have left himself at home and brought back somebody else: whether or not, the boy certainly improved, so that there was less occasion to find fault with him afterward.

Jess lived to be quite an old pony, and carried a great many people—little people always, for she herself never grew any bigger. But I don't think she ever carried a Brownie again.

Adventure the Fifth
Brownie on the Ice

Winter was a grand time with the six little children especially when they had frost and snow. This happened seldom enough for it to be the greatest possible treat when it did happen; and it never lasted very long, for the winters are warm in Devonshire.

There was a little lake three fields off, which made the most splendid sliding-place imaginable. No skaters went near it—it was not large enough; and besides, there was nobody to skate, the neighborhood being lonely. The lake itself looked the loneliest place imaginable. It was not very deep—not deep enough to drown a man—but it had a gravelly bottom, and was always very clear. Also, the trees round it grew so thick that they sheltered it completely from the wind, so, when it did freeze, it generally froze as smooth as a sheet of glass.

"The lake bears!" was such a grand event, and so rare, that when it did occur, the news came at once to the farm, and the children carried it as quickly to their mother. For she had promised them that, if such a thing did happen this year—it did not happen every year—lessons should be stopped entirely, and they should all go down to the lake and slide, if they liked, all day long.

So one morning, just before Christmas, the eldest boy ran in with a countenance of great delight.

"Mother, mother, the lake bears!" (It was rather a compliment to call it a lake, it being only about twenty yards across and forty long.) "The lake really bears!"

"Who says so?"

"Bill. Bill has been on it for an hour this morning, and has made us two such beautiful slides, he says—an upslide and a down-slide. May we go directly?"

The mother hesitated.

"You promised, you know," pleaded the children.

"Very well, then; only be careful."

"And may we slide all day long, and never come home for dinner or any thing?"

"Yes, if you like. Only Gardener must go with you, and stay all day."

This they did not like at all; nor, when Gardener was spoken to, did he.

"You bothering children! I wish you may all get a good ducking in the lake! Serve you right for making me lose a day's work, just to look after you little monkeys. I've a great mind to tell your mother I won't do it."

But he did not, being fond of his mistress. He was also fond of his work, but he had no notion of play. I think the saying of, "All work and no play makes Jack a dull boy," must have been applied to him, for Gardener, whatever he had been as a boy, was certainly a dull and melancholy man. The children used to say that if he and idle Bill could have been kneaded into one, and baked in the oven—a very warm oven—they would have come out rather a pleasant person.

As it was, Gardener was any thing but a pleasant person; above all, to spend a long day with, and on the ice, where one needs all one's cheerfulness and good-humor to bear pinched fingers and numbed toes, and trips and tumbles, and various uncomfortablenesses.

"He'll growl at us all day long—he'll be a regular spoil-sport!" lamented the children. "Oh! mother, mightn't we go alone?"

"No!" said the mother; and her "No" meant no, though she was always very kind. They argued the point no more, but started off, rather downhearted. But soon they regained their spirits, for it was a bright, clear, frosty day—the sun shining, though not enough to melt the ice, and just sufficient to lie like a thin sprinkling over the grass, and turn the brown branches into white ones. The little people danced along to keep themselves warm, carrying between them a basket which held their lunch. A very harmless lunch it was—just a large brown loaf and a lump of cheese, and a knife to cut it with. Tossing the basket about in their fun, they managed to tumble the knife out, and were having a search for it in the long grass, when Gardener came up, grumpily enough.

"To think of trusting you children with one of the table-knives and a basket! what a fool Cook must be! I'll tell her so; and if they're lost she'll blame me: give me the things."

He put the knife angrily in one pocket. "Perhaps it will cut a hole in it," said one of the children, in rather a pleased tone than otherwise; then he turned the lunch all out on the grass and crammed it in the other pocket, hiding the basket behind a hedge.

"I'm sure I'll not be at the trouble of carrying it," said he, when the children cried out at this; "and you shan't carry it either, for you'll knock it about and spoil it. And as for your lunch getting warm in my pocket, why, so much the better this cold day."

It was not a lively joke, and they knew the pocket was very dirty; indeed, the little girls had seen him stuff a dead rat into it only the day before. They looked ready to cry; but there was no help for them, except going back and complaining to their mother, and they did not like to do that. Besides, they knew that, though Gardener was cross, he was trustworthy, and she would never let them go down to the lake without him.

So they followed him, trying to be as good as they could—though it was difficult work. One of them proposed pelting him with snowballs, as they pelted each other. But at the first—which fell in his neck—he turned round so furiously, that they never sent a second, but walked behind him as meek as mice.

As they went, they heard little steps pattering after them.

"Perhaps it is the Brownie to play with us—I wish he would," whispered the youngest girl to the eldest boy, whose hand she generally held; and then the little pattering steps sounded again, traveling through the snow, but they saw nobody—so they said nothing.

The children would have liked to go straight to the ice; but Gardener insisted on taking them a mile round, to look at an extraordinary animal which a farmer there had just got—sent by his brother in Australia. The two old men stood gossiping so long that the children wearied extremely. Every minute seemed an hour till they got on the ice.

At last one of them pulled Gardener's coat-tails, and whispered that they were quite ready to go.

"Then I'm not," and he waited ever so much longer, and got a drink of hot cider, which made him quite lively for a little while.

But by the time they reached the lake, he was as cross as ever. He struck the ice with his stick, but made no attempt to see if it really did bear—though he would not allow the children to go one step upon it till he had tried.

"I know it doesn't bear, and you'll just have to go home again—a good thing too—saves me from losing a day's work."

"Try, only try; Bill said it bore," implored the boys, and looked wistfully at the two beautiful slides—just as Bill said, one up and one down—stretching all across the lake; "of course it bears, or Bill could not have made these slides."

"Bill's an ass!" said the Gardener, and put his heavy foot cautiously on the ice. Just then there was seen jumping across it a creature which certainly had never been seen on ice before. It made the most extraordinary bounds on its long hind legs, with its little fore legs tucked up in front of it as if it wanted to carry a muff; and its long, stiff tail sticking out straight behind, to balance it itself with apparently. The children at first started with surprise, and then burst out laughing, for it was the funniest creature, and had the funniest way of getting along, that they had ever seen in their lives.

"It's the kangaroo!" said Gardener, in great excitement. "It has got loose—and it's sure to be lost—and what a way Mr. Giles will be in! I must go and tell him. Or stop, I'll try and catch it."

But in vain—it darted once or twice across the ice, dodging him, as it were; and once coming so close that he nearly caught it by the tail—to the children's great delight—then it vanished entirely.

Miss Mulock

"I must go and tell Mr. Giles directly," said Gardener, and then stopped. For he had promised not to leave the children; and it was such a wild-goose chase, after an escaped kangaroo. But he might get half a crown as a reward, and he was sure of another glass of cider.

"You just stop quiet here, and I'll be back in five minutes," said he to the children. "You may go a little way on the ice—I think it's sound enough; only mind you don't tumble in, for there'll be nobody to pull you out."

"Oh no," said the children, clapping their hands. They did not care for tumbling in, and were quite glad there was nobody there to pull them out. They hoped Gardener would stop a very long time away—only, as some one suggested when he was seen hurrying across the snowy field, he had taken away their lunch in his pocket, too.

Off they darted, the three elder boys, with a good run; the biggest of the girls followed after them; and soon the whole four were skimming one after the other, as fast as a railway train, across the slippery ice. And, like a railway train, they had a collision, and all came tumbling one over the other, with great screaming and laughing, to the high bank on the other side. The two younger ones stood mournfully watching the others from the opposite bank—when there stood beside them a small brown man.

"Ho-ho! little people," said he, coming between them and taking hold of a hand of each. His was so warm and theirs so cold, that it was quite comfortable. And then, somehow, they found in their mouths a nice lozenge—I think it was peppermint, but am not sure; which comforted them still more.

"Did you want me to play with you?" cried the Brownie; "then here I am. What shall we do? Have a turn on the ice together?"

No sooner said than done. The two children felt themselves floating along—it was more like floating than running—with Brownie between them; up the lake, and down the lake, and across the lake, not at all interfering with the sliders—indeed, it was a great deal better than sliding. Rosy and breathless, their toes so nice and warm, and their hands feeling like mince-pies just taken out of the oven—the little ones came to a standstill.

The elder ones stopped their sliding, and looked toward Brownie with entreating eyes. He swung himself up to a willow bough, and then turned head over heels on to the ice.

"Halloo! you don't mean to say you big ones want a race too! Well, come along—if the two eldest will give a slide to the little ones."

He watched them take a tiny sister between them, and slide her up one slide

The two little children felt themselves floating along—with Brownie between them

and down another, screaming with delight. Then he took the two middle children in either hand.

"One, two, three, and away!" Off they started—scudding along as light as feathers and as fast as steam-engines, over the smooth, black ice, so clear that they could see the bits of stick and water-grasses frozen in it, and even the little fishes swimming far down below—if they had only looked long enough.

When all had had their fair turns, they began to be frightfully hungry.

"Catch a fish for dinner, and I'll lend you a hook," said Brownie. At which they all laughed, and then looked rather grave. Pulling a cold, raw live fish from under the ice and eating it was not a pleasant idea of dinner. "Well, what would you like to have? Let the little one choose."

She said, after thinking a minute, that she should like a currant-cake.

"And I'd give all you a bit of it—a very large bit—I would indeed!" added she, almost with the tears in her eyes—she was so very hungry.

"Do it, then!" said the Brownie, in his little squeaking voice.

Immediately the stone that the little girl was sitting on—a round, hard stone, and so cold!—turned into a nice hot cake—so hot that she jumped up directly. As soon as she saw what it was, she clapped her hands for joy.

"Oh, what a beautiful, beautiful cake! only we haven't got a knife to cut it."

The boys felt in all their pockets, but somehow their knives never were there when they were wanted.

"Look! you've got one in your hand!" said Brownie to the little one; and that minute a bit of stick she held turned into a bread-knife—silver, with an ivory handle—big enough and sharp enough, without being too sharp. For the youngest girl was not allowed to use sharp knives, though she liked cutting things excessively, especially cakes.

"That will do. Sit you down and carve the dinner. Fair shares and don't let any body eat too much. Now begin, ma'am," said the Brownie, quite politely, as if she had been ever so old.

Oh, how proud the little girl was. How bravely she set to work, and cut five of the biggest slices you ever saw, and gave them to her brothers and sisters, and was just going to take the sixth slice for herself, when she remembered the Brownie.

"I beg your pardon," said she, as politely as he, though she was such a very little girl, and turned round to the wee brown man. But he was nowhere to be seen. The slices of cake in the children's hands remained cake, and uncommonly good it was, and such substantial eating that it did nearly the same as dinner; but the cake itself turned suddenly to a stone again, and the knife into a bit of stick.

For there was the Gardener coming clumping along by the bank of the lake, and growling as he went.

"Have you got the kangaroo?" shouted the children, determined to be civil, if possible.

"This place is bewitched, I think," said he, "The kangaroo was fast asleep in the cow-shed. What! how dare you laugh at me?"

But they hadn't laughed at all. And they found it no laughing matter, poor children, when Gardener came on the ice, and began to scold them and order them about. He was perfectly savage with crossness; for the people at Giles's Farm had laughed at him very much, and he did not like to be laughed at—and at the top of the field he had by chance met his mistress, and she asked him severely how he could think of leaving the children alone.

Altogether, his conscience pricked him a good deal, and when people's consciences prick them, sometimes they get angry with other people, which is very silly, and only makes matters worse.

"What have you been doing all this time?" said he.

"All this five minutes?" said the oldest boy, mischievously; for Gardener was only to be away five minutes, and he had staid a full hour. Also, when he fumbled in his pocket for the children's lunch—to stop their tongues, perhaps—he found it was not there.

They set up a great outcry; for, in spite of the cake, they could have eaten a little more. Indeed, the frost had such an effect upon all their appetites, that they felt not unlike that celebrated gentleman of whom it is told that

> "He ate a cow, and ate a calf,
> He ate an ox, and ate a half;
> He ate a church, he ate the steeple,
> He ate the priest, and all the people,
> And said he hadn't had enough then."

"We're so hungry, so very hungry! Couldn't you go back again and fetch us some dinner?" cried they, entreatingly.

"Not I, indeed. You may go back to dinner yourselves. You shall, indeed, for I want my dinner too. Two hours is plenty long enough to stop on the ice."

"It isn't two hours—it's only one."

"Well, one will do better than more. You're all right now—and you might soon tumble in, or break your legs on the slide. So come away home."

It wasn't kind of Gardener, and I don't wonder the children felt it hard; indeed, the eldest boy resisted stoutly.

"Mother said we might stop all day, and we will stop all day. You may go home if you like."

"I won't, and you shall!" said Gardener, smacking a whip that he carried in his hand. "Stop till I catch you, and I'll give you this about your back, my fine gentleman."

And he tried to follow, but the little fellow darted across the ice, objecting to be either caught or whipped. It may have been rather naughty, but I am afraid it was great fun dodging the Gardener up and down; he being too timid to go on the slippery ice, and sometimes getting so close that the whip nearly touched the lad.

"Bless us! there's the kangaroo again!" said he, starting. Just as he had caught the boy, and lifted the whip, the creature was seen hop-hopping from bank to bank. "I can't surely be mistaken this time; I must catch it."

Which seemed quite easy, for it limped as if it was lame, or as if the frost had bitten its toes, poor beast! Gardener went after it, walking cautiously on the slippery, crackling ice, and never minding whether or not he walked on the slides, though they called out to him that his nailed boots would spoil them.

But whether it was that ice which bears a boy will not bear a man, or whether at each lame step of the kangaroo there came a great crack, is more than I can tell. However, just as Gardener reached the middle of the lake, the ice suddenly broke, and in he popped.—The kangaroo too, apparently, for it was not seen afterward.

What a hullaballoo the poor man made! Not that he was drowning—the lake was too shallow to drown any body, but he got terribly wet, and the water was very cold. He soon scrambled out, the boys helping him; and then he hobbled home as fast as he could, not even saying thank you, or taking the least notice of them.

Indeed, nobody took notice of them—nobody came to fetch them, and they might have staid sliding the whole afternoon.

Only somehow they did not feel quite easy in their minds. And though the hole in the ice closed up immediately, and it seemed as firm as ever, still they did not like to slide upon it again.

"I think we had better go home and tell mother every thing," said one of them. "Besides, we ought to see what has become of poor Gardener. He was very wet."

"Yes, but oh, how funny he looked!" And they all burst out laughing at the recollection of the figure he cut,

The ice suddenly broke, and in he popped.

scrambling out through the ice with his trowsers dripping up to the knees, and the water running out of his boots, making a little pool, wherever he stepped.

"And it freezes so hard, that by the time he gets home his clothes will be as stiff as a board. His wife will have to put him to the fire to thaw before he can get out of them."

Again the little people burst into shouts of laughter. Although they laughed, they were a little sorry for the poor old Gardener, and hoped no great harm had come to him, but that he had got safe home and been dried by his own warm fire.

The frosty mist was beginning already to rise, and the sun, though still high up in the sky, looked like a ball of red-hot iron as the six children went homeward across the fields—merry enough still, but not quite so merry as they had been a few hours before.

"Let's hope mother won't be vexed with us," said they, "but will let us come back again to-morrow. It wasn't our fault that Gardener tumbled in."

As somebody said this, they all heard quite distinctly, "Ha, ha, ha!" and "Ho, ho, ho!" and a sound of little steps pattering behind.

But whatever they thought, nobody ventured to say that it was the fault of the Brownie.

*Adventure the Sixth and Last
Brownie and the Clothes*

Till the next time; but when there is a Brownie in the house, no one can say that any of his tricks will be the last. For there's no stopping a Brownie, and no getting rid of him either. This one had followed the family from house to house, generation after generation—never any older, and sometimes seeming even to grow younger by the tricks he played. In fact, though he looked like an old man, he was a perpetual child.

To the children he never did any harm, quite the contrary. And his chief misdoings were against those who vexed the children. But he gradually made friends with several of his grown up enemies. Cook, for instance, who had ceased to be lazy at night and late in the morning, found no more black footmarks on her white table cloth. And Brownie found his basin of milk waiting for him, night after night, behind the coal-cellar door.

Bill, too, got on well enough with his pony, and Jess was taken no more night-rides. No ducks were lost; and Dolly gave her milk quite comfortably to whoever milked her. Alas! this was either Bill or the Gardener's wife now. After that adventure on the ice, poor Gardener very seldom appeared; when he did, it was on two crutches, for he had had rheumatism in his feet, and could not stir outside his cottage door. Bill, therefore, had double work; which was probably all the better for Bill.

The garden had to take care of itself; but this being winter-time, it did not much signify. Besides, Brownie seldom went into the garden, except in summer; during the hard weather he preferred to stop in his coal-cellar. It might not have been a lively place, but it was warm, and he liked it.

He had company there, too; for when the cat had more kittens—the kitten he used to tease being grown up now—they were all put in a hamper in the coal-cellar; and of cold nights Brownie used to jump in beside them, and be as warm and as cozy as a kitten himself. The little things never were heard to mew; so it may be supposed they liked his society. And the old mother-cat evidently bore him no malice for the whipping she had got by mistake; so Brownie must have found means of coaxing her over. One thing you may be sure of—all the while she and her kittens were in his coal-cellar, he took care never to turn himself into a mouse.

He was spending the winter, on the whole, very comfortably, without much trouble either to himself or his neighbors, when one day, the coal-cellar being nearly empty, two men, and a great wagon-load of coals behind them, came to the door, Gardener's wife following.

"My man says you're to give the cellar a good cleaning out before you put any more in," said she, in her sharp voice; "and don't be lazy about it. It'll not take you ten minutes, for it's nearly all coal-dust, except that one big lump in the corner— you might clear that out too."

"Stop, it's the Brownie's lump! better not meddle with it," whispered the little scullery-maid.

"Don't you meddle with matters that can't concern you," said the Gardener's wife, who had been thinking what a nice help it would be to her fire. To be sure, it was not her lump of coal, but she thought she might take it; the mistress would never miss it, or the Brownie either. He must be a very silly old Brownie to live under a lump of coal.

So she argued with herself, and made the men lift it. "You must lift it, you see, if you are to sweep the coal-cellar out clean. And you may as well put it on the barrow, and I'll wheel it out of your way."

This she said in quite a civil voice, lest they should tell of her, and stood by while it was being done. It was done without any thing happening, except that a large rat ran out of the coal-cellar door, bouncing against her feet, and frightening her so much that she nearly tumbled down.

"See what nonsense it is to talk of Brownies living in a coal-cellar. Nothing lives there but rats, and I'll have them poisoned pretty soon, and get rid of them."

But she was rather frightened all the same, for the rat had been such a very big rat, and had looked at her, as it darted past, with such wild, bright, mischievous eyes—brown eyes, of course—that she all but jumped with surprise.

However, she had got her lump of coal, and was wheeling it quietly away, nobody seeing, to her cottage at the bottom of the garden. She was a hard-worked woman, and her husband's illness made things harder for her. Still, she was not quite easy at taking what did not belong to her.

"I don't suppose any body will miss the coal," she repeated. "I dare say the mistress would have given it to me if I had asked her; and as for its being the Brownie's lump—fudge! Bless us! what's that?"

For the barrow began to creak dreadfully, and every creak sounded like the cry of a child, just as if the wheel were going over its leg and crushing its poor little bones.

"What a horrid noise! I must grease the barrow. If only I knew where they keep the grease-box. All goes wrong, now my old man's laid up. Oh, dear! oh dear!"

For suddenly the barrow had tilted over, though there was not a single stone near, and the big coal was tumbled on to the ground, where it broke into a thousand pieces. Gathering it up again was hopeless, and it made such a mess on the gravel-walk, that the old woman was thankful her misfortune happened behind the privet hedge, where nobody was likely to come.

"I'll take a broom and sweep it up to-morrow. Nobody goes near the orchard now, except me when I hang out the clothes; so I need say nothing about it to the old man or any body. But ah! deary me, what a beautiful lot of coal I've lost!"

She stood and looked at it mournfully, and then went into her cottage, where she found two or three of the little children keeping Gardener company. They did not dislike to do this now; but he was so much kinder than he used to be—so quiet and patient, though he suffered very much. And he had never once reproached them for what they always remembered—how it was ever since he was on the ice with them that he had got the rheumatism.

So, one or other of them made a point of going to see him every day, and telling him all the funny things they could think of—indeed, it was a contest among them who should first make Gardener laugh. They did not succeed in doing that exactly; but they managed to make him smile; and he was always gentle and grateful to them; so that they sometimes thought it was rather nice his being ill.

But his wife was not pleasant; she grumbled all day long, and snapped at him and his visitors; being especially snappish this day, because she had lost her big coal.

"I can't have you children come bothering here," said she, crossly. "I want to wring out my clothes, and hang them to dry. Be off with you!"

"Let us stop a little—just to tell Gardener this one curious thing about Dolly and the pig—and then we'll help you to take your clothes to the orchard; we can carry your basket between us—we can, indeed."

That was the last thing the woman wished; for she knew the that the children would be sure to see the mess on the gravel-walk—and they were such inquisitive children—they noticed every thing. They would want to know all about it, and how the bits of coal came there. It was very a awkward position. But people who take other people's property often do find themselves in awkward positions.

"Thank you, young gentlemen," said she, quite politely; "but indeed the basket is too heavy for you. However, you may stop and gossip a little longer with my old man. He likes it."

And, while they were shut up with Gardener in his bedroom, off she went, carrying the basket on her head, and hung her clothes carefully out—the big things on lines between the fruit trees, and the little things, such as stockings and pocket handkerchiefs, stuck on the gooseberry-bushes, or spread upon the clean green grass.

"Such a fine day as it is! they'll dry directly," said she, cheerfully, to herself. "Plenty of sun, and not a breath of wind to blow them about. I'll leave them for an hour or two, and come and fetch them in before it grows dark. Then I shall get all my folding done by bedtime, and have a clear day for ironing to-morrow."

But when she did fetch them in, having bundled them all together in the dusk of the evening, never was such a sight as those clothes! They were all twisted in the oddest way—the stockings turned inside out, with the heels and toes tucked into the legs; the sleeves of the shirts tied together in double knots, the pocket-handkerchiefs made into round balls, so tight that if you had pelted a person with them they would have given very hard blows indeed. And the whole looked as if, instead of lying quietly on the grass and bushes, they had been dragged through heaps of mud and then stamped upon, so that there was not a clean inch upon them from end to end.

"What a horrid mess!" cried the Gardener's wife, who had been at first very angry, and then very frightened. "But I know what it is; that nasty Boxer has got loose again. It's he that has done it."

"Boxer wouldn't tie shirt-sleeves in double knots, or make balls of pocket-handkerchiefs," Gardener was heard to answer, solemnly.

"Then it's those horrid children; they are always up to some mischief or other—just let me catch them!"

"You'd better not," said somebody in a voice exactly like Gardener's, though he himself declared he had not spoken a word. Indeed, he was fast asleep.

"Well, it's the most extraordinary thing I ever heard of," the Gardener's wife said, supposing she was talking to her husband all the time; but soon she held her tongue, for she found here and there among the clothes all sorts of queer marks—marks of fingers, and toes, and heels, not in mud at all, but in coal-dust, as black as black could be.

Now, as the place where the big coal had tumbled out of the barrow was fully fifty yards from the orchard, and, as the coal could not come to the clothes, and the clothes could not go without hands, the only conclusion she could arrive at was—well, no particular conclusion at all!

It was too late that night to begin washing again; besides, she was extremely tired, and her husband woke up rather worse than usual, so she just bundled the clothes up anyhow in a corner, put the kitchen to rights, and went mournfully to bed.

Next morning she got up long before it was light, washed her clothes through all over again, and, it being impossible to dry them by the fire, went out with them once more, and began spreading them out in their usual corner, in a hopeless and melancholy manner. While she was at it, the little folks came trooping around her. She didn't scold them this time, she was too low-spirited.

"No! my old man isn't any better, and I don't fancy he ever will be," said she, in answer to their questions. "And every thing's going wrong with us—just listen!" And she told the trick which had been played her about the clothes.

The little people tried not to laugh, but it was so funny; and even now, the minute she had done hanging them out, there was something so droll in the way the clothes blew about, without any wind; the shirts hanging with their necks downward, as if there was a man inside them; and the drawers standing stiffly astride on the gooseberry-bushes, for all the world as if they held a pair of legs still. As for Gardener's night-caps—long, white cotton, with a tassel at the top—they were alarming to look at; just like a head stuck on the top of a pole.

The whole thing was so peculiar, and the old woman so comical in her despair, that the children, after trying hard to keep it in, at last broke into shouts of laughter. She turned furiously upon them.

"It was you who did it!"

"No, indeed it wasn't!" said they, jumping farther to escape her blows. For she had got one of her clothes-props, and was laying about her in the most reckless manner. However, she hurt nobody, and then she suddenly burst out, not laughing, but crying.

"It's a cruel thing, whoever has done it, to play such tricks on a poor old body like me, with a sick husband that she works hard for, and not a child to help her. But I don't care. I'll wash my clothes again, if it's twenty times over, and I'll hang them out again in the very place, just to make you all ashamed of yourselves."

Perhaps the little people were ashamed of themselves, though they really had not done the mischief. But they knew quite well who had done it, and more than once they were about to tell; only they were afraid, if they did so, they should vex the Brownie so much that he would never come and play with them any more.

So they looked at one another without speaking, and when the Gardener's wife had emptied her basket and dried her eyes, they said to her, very kindly:

"Perhaps no harm may come to your clothes this time. We'll sit and watch them till they are dry."

"Just as you like; I don't care. Them that hides can find, and them that plays tricks knows how to stop 'em."

It was not a civil speech, but then things were hard for the poor old woman. She had been awake nearly all night, and up washing at daybreak; her eyes were red with crying, and her steps weary and slow. The little children felt quite sorry for her, and, instead of going to play, sat watching the clothes as patiently as possible.

Nothing came near them. Sometimes, as before, the things seemed to dance about without hands, and turn into odd shapes, as if there were people inside them; but not a creature was seen and not a sound was heard. And though there was neither wind nor sun, very soon all the linen was perfectly dry.

"Fetch one of mother's baskets, and we'll fold it up as tidily as possible—that is, the girls can do it, it's their business—and we boys will carry it safe to Gardener's cottage."

So said they, not liking to say that they could not trust it out of their sight for fear of Brownie, whom, indeed, they were expecting to see peer round from every bush. They began to have a secret fear that he was rather a naughty Brownie; but then, as the eldest little girl whispered, "He was only a Brownie, and knew no better." Now they were growing quite big children, who would be men and women some time; when they hoped they would never do any thing wrong. (Their parents hoped the same, but doubted it.)

In a serious and careful manner they folded up the clothes, and laid them one by one in the basket without any mischief, until, just as the two biggest boys were lifting their burden to carry it away, they felt something tugging at it from underneath.

"Halloo! Where are you taking all this rubbish? Better give it to me."

"No, if you please," said they, very civilly, not to offend the little brown man. "We'll not trouble you, thanks! We'd rather do it ourselves; for poor Gardener is very ill, and his wife is very miserable, and we are extremely sorry for them both."

"Extremely sorry!" cried Brownie, throwing up his cap in the air, and tumbling head over heels in an excited manner. "What in the world does extremely sorry mean?"

The children could not explain, especially to a Brownie; but they thought they understood—anyhow, they felt it. And they looked so sorrowful that the Brownie could not tell what to make of it.

He could not be said to be sorry, since, being a Brownie, and not a human being, knowing right from wrong, he never tried particularly to do right, and had no idea that he was doing wrong. But he seemed to have an idea that he was troubling the children, and he never liked to see them look unhappy.

So he turned head over heels six times running, and then came back again.

"The silly old woman! I washed her clothes for her last night in a way she didn't expect. I hadn't any soap, so I used a little mud and coal-dust, and very pretty they looked. Ha, ha, ha! Shall I wash them over again to-night?"

"Oh, no, please don't!" implored the children.

"Shall I starch and iron them? I'll do it beautifully. One—two—three, five—six—seven, Abracadabra, tum—tum—ti!" shouted he, jabbering all sorts of nonsense, as it seemed to the children, and playing such antics that they stood and stared in the utmost amazement, and quite forgot the clothes. When they looked round again, the basket was gone.

"Seek till you find, seek till you find,
Under the biggest gooseberry-bush, exactly to your mind."

They heard him singing this remarkable rhyme, long after they had lost sight of him. And then they all set about searching; but it was a long while before they found, and still longer before they could decide, which was the biggest gooseberry-bush, each child having his or her opinion— sometimes a very strong one—on the matter. At last they agreed to settle it by pulling half-a-dozen little sticks, to see which stick was the longest, and the child that held it was to decide the gooseberry-bush.

This done, underneath the branches what should they find but the identical basket of clothes! only, instead of being roughly dried, they were all starched and ironed in the most beautiful manner. As for the shirts, they really were a picture to behold, and the stockings were all folded up, and even darned in one or two places, as neatly as possible. And strange to tell, there was not a single black mark of feet or fingers on any one of them.

"Kind little Brownie! clever little Brownie!" cried the children in chorus, and thought this was the most astonishing trick he had ever played.

What the Gardener's wife said about it, whether they told her any thing, or allowed her to suppose that the clothes had been done in their own laundry instead of the Brownie's (wherever that establishment might be), is more than I can tell. Of one thing only I am certain—that the little people said nothing but what was true. Also, that the very minute they got home they told their mother every thing.

But for a long time after that they were a good deal troubled. Gardener got better, and went hobbling about the place again, to his own and every body's great content, and his wife was less sharp-tongued and complaining than usual— indeed, she had nothing to complain of. All the family were very flourishing, except the little Brownie.

Often there was heard a curious sound all over the house; it might have been rats squeaking behind the wainscot—the elders said it was—but the children were sure it was a sort of weeping and wailing.

"They've stolen my coal,
And I haven't a hole
To hide in;
Not even a house
One could ask a mouse
To bide in."

A most forlorn tune it was, ending in a dreary minor key, and it lasted for months and months—at least the children said it did. And they were growing quite dull for want of a playfellow, when, by the greatest good luck in the world, there came to the house not only a new lot of kittens, but a new baby. And the new baby was everybody's pet, including the Brownie's.

From that time, though he was not often seen, he was continually heard up and down the staircase, where he was frequently mistaken for Tiny or the cat, and sent sharply down again, which was wasting a great deal of wholesome anger upon Mr. Nobody. Or he lurked in odd corners of the nursery, whither the baby was seen crawling eagerly after nothing in particular, or sitting laughing with all her might at something— probably her own toes.

But, as Brownie was never seen, he was never suspected. And since he did no mischief—neither pinched the baby nor broke the toys, left no soap in the bath and no footmarks about the room—but was always a well-conducted Brownie in every way, he was allowed to inhabit the nursery (or supposed to do so, since, as nobody saw him, nobody could prevent him), until the children were grown up into men and women.

After that he retired into his coal-cellar, and, for all I know, he may live there still, and have gone through hundreds of adventures since; but as I never heard them, I can't tell them. Only I think, if I could be a little child again, I should exceedingly like a Brownie to play with me. Should not you?

The Blackbird And The Rooks.

A slender young Blackbird built in a thorn-tree
A spruce little fellow as ever could be;
His bill was so yellow, his feathers so black,
So long was his tail, and so glossy his back,
That good Mrs. B., who sat hatching her eggs,
And only just left them to stretch her poor legs,
And pick for a minute the worm she preferred,
Thought there never was seen such a beautiful bird.

And such a kind husband! how early and late
He would sit at the top of the old garden gate,
And sing, just as merry as if it were June,
Being ne'er out of patience, or temper, or tune.
"So unlike those Rooks, dear; from morning till night
They seem to do nothing but quarrel and fight,
And wrangle and jangle, and plunder—while we
Sit, honest and safe, in our pretty thorn-tree."

Just while she was speaking, a lively young Rook
Alit with a flap that the thorn-bush quite shook,
And seizing a stick from the nest—"Come, I say,
That will just suit me, neighbor"—flew with it away
The lady loud twittered—her husband soon heard:
Though peaceful, he was not a cowardly bird;
And with arguments angry enough to o'erwhelm
A whole Rookery—flew to the top of the elm.

"How dare you, you—" (thief he was going to say;
But a civiller sentiment came in the way:
For he knew 'tis no good, and it anyhow shames
A gentleman, calling strange gentlemen names:)
"Pray what is your motive, Sir Rook, for such tricks,
As building your mansion with other folks' sticks?
I request you'll restore them, in justice and law."
At which the whole colony set up a—caw!

But Blackbird, not silenced, then spoke out again;
"I've built my small nest with much labor and pain.
I'm a poor singing gentleman, Sirs, it is true,
Though cockneys do often mistake me for you;

But I keep Mrs. Blackbird, and four little eggs,
And neither e'er pilfers, or borrows, or begs.
Now have I not right on my side, do you see?"
But they flew at and pecked him all down the elm-tree.

Ah! wickedness prospers sometimes, I much fear;
And virtue's not always victorious, that's clear:
At least, not at first: for it must be confessed
Poor Blackbird lost many a stick from his nest;
And his unkind grand neighbors with scoffing caw-caws,
In his voice and his character found many flaws,
And jeered him and mocked him; but when they'd all done,
He flew to his tree and sang cheerily on.

At length May arrived with her garlands of leaves;
The swallows were building beneath the farm-eaves,
Wrens, linnets, and sparrows, on every hedge-side,
Were bringing their families out with great pride;
While far above all, on the tallest tree-top,
With a flutter and clamor that never did stop,
The haughty old Rooks held their heads up so high,
And dreamed not of trouble—until it drew nigh!

One morning at seven, as he came with delight
To his wife's pretty parlor of may-blossoms white,
Having fed all his family ere rise of sun,—
Mr. Blackbird perceived—a big man with a gun;
Who also perceived him: "See, Charlie, among
That may, sits the Blackbird we've heard for so long:
Most likely his nest's there—how frightened he looks!
Nay, Blackie, we're not come for you, but the Rooks."

I don't say 'twas cruel—I can't say 'twas kind—
On the subject I haven't quite made up my mind:
But those guns went pop-popping all morning, alas!
And young Rooks kept dropping among the long grass,
Till good Mr. Blackbird, who watched the whole thing,
For pity could scarcely a single note sing,
And in the May sunset he hardly could bear
To hear the returning Rooks' caw of despair.

"O, dear Mrs. Blackbird," at last warbled he,
"How happy we are in our humble thorn-tree;

How gaily we live, living honest and poor,
How sweet are the may-blossoms over our door."
"And then our dear children," the mother replied,
And she nested them close to her warm feathered side,
And with a soft twitter of drowsy content,
In the quiet May moonlight to sleep they all went.

The Shaking Of The Pear-Tree

Of all days I remember,
In summers passed away,
Was "the shaking of the pear-tree,"
In grandma's orchard gay.

A large old-fashioned orchard,
With long grass under foot,
And blackberry-brambles crawling
In many a tangled shoot.

From cherry time, till damsons
Dropped from the branches sere,
That wonderful old orchard
Was full of fruit all year;

We pick'd it up in baskets,
Or pluck'd it from the wall;
But the shaking of the pear-tree
Was the grandest treat of all.

Long, long the days we counted
Until that day drew nigh;
Then, how we watched the sun set,
And criticised the sky!

If rain—"'Twill clear at midnight;"
If dawn broke chill and gray,
"O many a cloudy morning
Turns out a lovely day."

So off we started gaily,
Heedless of jolt or jar;
Through town and lane, and hamlet,
In old Llewellyn's car.

He's dead and gone—Llewellyn,
These twenty years, I doubt:
If I put him in this poem,
He'll never find it out,

The patient, kind Llewellyn—
Whose broad face smiled all o'er,
As he lifted out us children
At grandma's very door.

And there stood Grandma's Betty,
With cheeks like apples red;
And Dash, the spaniel, waddled
Out of his cosy bed.

With silky ears down dropping,
And coat of chestnut pale;
He was so fat and lazy
He scarce could wag his tail.

Poor Dash is dead, and buried
Under the lilac-tree;
And Betty's old,—as, children,
We all may one day be.

I hope no child will vex us,
As we vexed Betty then,
With winding up the draw-well,
Or hunting the old hen.

And teasing, teasing, teasing,
Till afternoon wore round,
And shaken pears came tumbling
In showers upon the ground.

O how we jumped and shouted!
O how we plunged amid
The long grass, where the treasures,
Dropped down and deftly hid;

Long, slender-shaped, red-russet,
Or yellow just like gold;
Ah! never pears have tasted
Like those sweet pears of old!

We ate—I'd best not mention
How many: paused to fill
Big basket after basket;

Working with right good-will;

Then hunted round the orchard
For half-ripe plums—in vain;
So, back unto the pear-tree,
To eat, and eat again.

I'm not on my confession,
And therefore need not say
How tired, and cross, and sleepy,
Some were ere close of day;

For pleasure has its ending,
And eke its troubles too;
Which you'll find out, my children,
As well as we could do.

But yet this very minute,
I seem to see it all—
The pear-tree's empty branches
The gray of evening-fall;

The children's homeward silence,
The furnace fires that glowed,
Each mile or so, out streaming
Across the lonely road;

And high, high set in heaven,
One large bright, beauteous star,
That shone between the curtains
Of old Llewellyn's car.

The Wonderful Apple-Tree.[1]

Come here, my dear boys, and I'll tell you a fable,
Which you may believe as much as you're able;
It isn't all true, nor all false, I'll be bound—
Of the tree that bears apples all the year round.

There was a Dean Tucker of Gloster city,
Who may have been wise, or worthy, or witty;
But I know nothing of him, the more's the pity,
Save that he was Dean Tucker of Gloster city.

And walking one day with a musing air
In his Deanery garden, close by where
The great cathedral's west window's seen,—
"I'll plant an apple," said Tucker the Dean.

The apple was planted, the apple grew,
A stout young tree, full of leaves not few;
The apple was grafted, the apple bore
Of goodly apples, one, two, three, four.

The old Dean walked in his garden fair,
"I'm glad I planted that young tree there,
Though it was but a shoot, or some old tree's sucker;
I'll taste it to-morrow," said good Dean Tucker.

But lo, in the night when (they say) trees talk,
And some of the liveliest get up and walk,
With fairies abroad for watch and warden—
There was such a commotion in the Dean's garden!

"I will not be gathered," the apple-tree said,
"Was it for this I blossomed so red?
Hung out my fruit all the summer days,
Got so much sunshine, and pleasure and praise?"

"Ah!" interrupted a solemn red plum,

_____

[1] This tree, known among gardeners by the name of "Winter-hanger" or
"Forbidden Fruit," was planted by Dean Tucker in 1760. It, or an off shoot
from it, still exists in the city of Gloucester.

Miss Mulock

"This is the end to which all of us come;
Last month I was laden with hundreds—but now"—
And he sighed the last little plum off from his bough.

"Nay, friend, take it easy," the pear-tree replied
(A lady-like person against the wall-side).
"Man guards, nurtures, trains us from top down to root:
I think 'tis but fair we should give him our fruit."

"No, I'll not be gathered," the apple resumed,
And shook his young branches, and fluttered and fumed;
"And I'll not drop neither, as some of you drop,
Over-ripe: I'm determined to keep my whole crop.

"And I with"—O'er his branches just then *something* flew;
It seemed like moth, large and grayish of hue.
But it was a Fairy. Her voice soft did sound,
"Be the tree that bears apples all the year round."

The Dean to his apple-tree, came, full of hope,
But tough was the fruit-stalk as double-twist rope,
And when he had cut it with patience and pain,
He bit just one mouthful—and never again.

"An apple so tasteless, so juiceless, so hard,
Is, sure, good for nought but to bowl in the yard;
The choir-boys may have it." But choir-boys soon found
It was worthless—the tree that bore all the year round.

And Gloster lads climbing the Deanery wall
Were punished, as well might all young thieves appal,
For, clutching the booty for which they did sin,
They bit at the apples—and left their teeth in!

And thus all the year from October till May,
From May till October, the apples shone gay;
But 'twas just outside glitter, for no hand was found
To pluck at the fruit which hung all the year round.

And so till they rotted, those queer apples hung,
The bare boughs and blossoms and ripe fruit among
And in Gloster city it still may be found—
The tree that bears apples all the year round.

~ 66 ~

The Jealous Boy

What, my little foolish Ned,
Think you mother's eyes are blind,
That her heart has grown unkind,
And she will not turn her head,
Cannot see, for all her joy,
Her poor jealous little boy?

What though sister be the pet—
Laughs, and leaps, and clings, and loves,
With her eyes as soft as dove's—
Why should yours with tears be wet?
Why such angry tears let fall?
Mother's heart has room for all.

Mother's heart is very wide,
And its doors all open stand:
Lightest touch of tiniest hand
She will never put aside.
Why her happiness destroy,
Foolish, naughty, jealous boy?

Come within the circle bright,
Where we laugh, and dance, and sing,
Full of love to everything;
As God loves us, day and night,
And *forgives* us. Come—with joy
Mother too forgives her boy.

Miss Mulock

The Story Of The Birkenhead
Told To Two Children

And so you want a fairy tale,
My little maidens twain?
Well, sit beside the waterfall,
Noisy with last night's rain;

On couch of moss, with elfin spears
Bristling, all fierce to see,
When from the yet brown moor down drops
The lonely April bee.

All the wide valley blushes green,
While, in far depths below,
Wharfe flashes out a great bright eye,
Then hides his shining flow;—

Wharfe, busy, restless, rapid Wharfe,
The glory of our dale;
O I could of the River Wharfe
Tell such a fairy tale!

"The Boy of Egremond," you cry,—
"And all the 'bootless bene:'
We know that poem, every word,
And we the Strid have seen."

No, clever damsels: though the tale
Seems still to bear a part,
In every lave of Wharfe's bright wave,
The broken mother's heart—

Little you know of broken hearts,
My Kitty, blithe and wise,
Grave Mary, with the woman soul
Dawning through childish eyes.

And long, long distant may God keep
The day when each shall know
The entrance to His kingdom through
His baptism of woe!

But yet 'tis good to hear of grief
Which He permits to be;
Even as in our green inland home
We talk of wrecks at sea.

So on this lovely day, when spring
Wakes soft o'er moor and dale,
I'll tell—not quite your wish—but yet
A noble "fairy" tale.

'Twas six o'clock in the morning,
The sea like crystal lay,
When the good troop-ship Birkenhead
Set sail from Simon's Bay.

The Cape of Good Hope on her right
Gloomed at her through the noon:
Brief tropic twilight fled, and night
Fell suddenly and soon.

At eight o'clock in the evening
Dim grew the pleasant land;
O'er smoothest seas the southern heaven
Its starry arch out-spanned.

The soldiers on the bulwarks leaned,
Smoked, chatted; and below
The soldiers' wives sang babes to sleep,
While on the ship sailed slow.

Six hundred and thirty souls held she,
Good, bad, old, young, rich, poor;
Six hundred and thirty living souls—
God knew them all.—Secure

He counted them in His right hand,
That held the hungering seas;
And to four hundred came a voice—
"The Master hath need of these."

On, onward, still the vessel went
Till, with a sudden shock,

Like one that's clutched by unseen Death,
She struck upon a rock.

She filled. Not hours, not minutes left;
Each second a life's gone:
Drowned in their berths, washed overboard,
Lost, swimming, one by one;

Till, o'er this chaos of despair
Rose, like celestial breath,
The law of order, discipline,
Obedience unto death.

The soldiers mustered upon deck,
As mute as on parade;
"Women and children to the boats!"
And not a man gainsayed.

Without a murmur or a moan
They stood, formed rank and file,
Between the dreadful crystal seas
And the sky's dreadful smile.

In face of death they did their work
As they in life would do,
Embarking at a quiet quay—
A quiet, silent crew.

"Now each man for himself. To the boats!"
Arose a passing cry.
The soldier-captain answered, "Swamp
The women and babes?—No, die!"

And so they died. Each in his place,
Obedient to command,
They went down with the sinking ship,
Went down in sight of land.

The great sea oped her mouth, and closed
O'er them. Awhile they trod
The valley of the shadow of death,
And then were safe with God.

My little girlies—What! your tears
Are dropping on the grass,
Over my more than "fairy" tale,
A tale that "really was!"

Nay, dry them. If we could but see
The joy in angels' eyes
O'er good lives, or heroic deaths
Of pure self-sacrifice,—

We should not weep o'er these that sleep—
Their short, sharp struggle o'er—
Under the rolling waves that break
Upon the Afric shore.

God works not as man works, nor sees
As man sees: though we mark
Ofttimes the moving of His hands
Beneath the eternal Dark.

But yet we know that all is well
That He, who loved all these,
Loves children laughing on the moor,
Birds singing in the trees;

That He who made both life and death,
He knoweth which is best:
We live to Him, we die to Him,
And leave Him all the rest.

Birds In The Snow

CHILD
I wish I were a little bird
When the sun shines
And the wind whispers low,
Through the tall pines,
I'd rock in the elm tops,
Rifle the pear-tree,
Hide in the cherry boughs,

O such a rare tree!
I wish I were a little bird;
All summer long
I'd fly so merrily
Sing such a song!
Song that should never cease
While daylight lasted,
Wings that should never tire
Howe'er they hasted.

       MOTHER
But if you were a little bird—
My baby-blossom.
Nestling so cosily
In mother's bosom,—
A bird, as we see them now,
When the snows harden,
And the wind's blighting breath
Howls round the garden:

What would you do, poor bird,
In winter drear?
No nest to creep into,
No mother near:
Hungry and desolate,
Weary and woeful,
All the earth bound with frost,
All the sky snow-full?

      CHILD (*thoughtfully*).
That would be sad, and yet

Hear what I'd do—
Mother, in winter time
I'd come to you!
If you can like the birds
Spite of their thieving,
Give them your trees to build,
Garden to live in,

I think if I were a bird
When winter comes
I'd trust you, mother dear,
For a few crumbs,
Whether I sang or not,
Were lark, thrush, or starling.—

MOTHER (*aside*).
Then—Father—I trust *Thee*
With this my darling.

Miss Mulock

The Little Comforter

"What is wrong with my big brother?"
Says the child;
For they two had got no mother
And she loved him like no other:
If he smiled,
All the world seemed bright and gay
To this happy little May.

If to her he sharply spoke,
This big brother—
Then her tender heart nigh broke;
But the cruel pain that woke,
She would smother—
As a little woman can;—
Was he not almost a man?

But when trouble or disgrace
Smote the boy,
She would lift her gentle face—
Surely 'twas her own right place.
To bring joy?
For she loved him—loved him so!
Whether he was good or no

May be he will never feel
Half her love;
Wound her, and forget to heal:
Idle words are sharp as steel:
But above,
I know what the angels say
Of this silent little May.

Don't Be Afraid.

Don't be afraid of the dark,
My daughter, dear as my soul!
You see but a part of the gloomy world,
But I—I have seen the whole,
And I know each step of the fearsome way,
Till the shadows brighten to open day.

Don't be afraid of pain,
My tender little child:
When its smart is worst there comes strength to bear,
And it seems as if angels smiled,—
As I smile, dear, when I hurt you now.
In binding up that wound on your brow.

Don't be afraid of grief,
'Twill come—as night follows day,
But the bleakest sky has tiny rifts
When the stars shine through—as to say
Wait, wait a little—till night is o'er
And beautiful day come back once more.

O child, be afraid of sin,
But have no other fear,
For God's in the dark, as well as the light;
And while we can feel Him near,
His hand that He gives, His love that He gave,
Lead safely, even to the dark of the grave.

Girl And Boy

Alfred is gentle as a girl,
But Judith longs to be a boy!
Would cut off every pretty curl
With eager joy!

Hates to be called "my dear"—or kissed:
For dollies does not care one fig:
Goes, sticking hands up to the wrist
In jackets big.

Would like to do whate'er boy can;
Play cricket—even to go school:
It is so grand to be a man!
A girl's a fool!

But Alfred smiles superior love
On all these innocent vagaries.
He'd hate a goose! but yet a dove
Ah, much more rare is!

She's anything but dove, good sooth!
But she's his dear and only sister:
And, had she been a boy, in truth
How he'd have missed her.

So, gradually her folly dies,
And she'll consent to be just human,
When there shines out of girlish eyes
The real Woman.

Agnes At Prayer

"Our Father which art in heaven,"
Little Agnes prays,
Though her kneeling is but show,
Though she is too young to know
All, or half she says.
God will hear her, Agnes mild,
God will love the innocent child.

"Our Father which art in heaven."
She has a father here,
Does she think of his kind eyes,
Tones that ne'er in anger rise—
"Yes, dear," or "No, dear."
They will haunt her whole life long
Like a sweet pathetic song.

"Our Father which art in heaven,"
Through thy peaceful prayer,
Think of the known father's face,
Of his bosom, happy place;
Safely sheltered there;
And so blessed—long may He bless!
Think too of the fatherless.

Going To Work

Come along for the work is ready—
Rough it may be, rough, tough and hard—
But—fourteen years old—stout, strong and steady,
Life's game's beginning, lad!—play your card—
Come along.

Mother stands at the door-step crying
Well but she has a brave heart too:
She'll try to be glad—there's nought like trying,
She's proud of having a son like you.
Come along.

Young as she is, her hair is whitening,
She has ploughed thro' years of sorrow deep,
She looks at her boy, and her eyes are brightening,
Shame if ever you make them weep!
Come along.

Bravo! See how the brown cheek flushes!
Ready to work as hard as you can?
I have always faith in a boy that blushes,
None will blush for him, when he's a man.
Come along.

Three Companions

We go on our way together,
Baby, and dog, and I;
Three merry companions,
'Neath any sort of sky;
Blue as her pretty eyes are,
Or gray, like his dear old tail;
Be it windy, or cloudy, or stormy,
Our courage does never fail.

Sometimes the snow lies thickly,
Under the hedge-row bleak;
Then baby cries "Pretty, pretty,"
The only word she can speak.
Sometimes two rivers of water
Run down the muddy lane;
Then dog leaps backwards and forwards
Barking with might and main.

Baby's a little lady,
Dog is a gentleman brave:
If he had two legs as you have
He'd kneel to her like a slave;
As it is he loves and protects her,
As dog and gentleman can;
I'd rather be a kind doggie
I think, than a brute of a man.

Miss Mulock

The Motherless Child

She was going home down the lonely street,
A widow-woman with weary feet
And weary eyes that seldom smiled:
She had neither mother, sister, nor child.
She earned her bread with a patient heart,
And ate it quietly and apart,
In her silent home from day to day,
No one to say her "ay," or "nay."

She was going home without care to haste;
What should she haste for? On she paced
Through the snowy night so bleak and wild,
When she thought she heard the cry of a child,
A feeble cry, not of hunger or pain,
But just of sorrow. It came again.
She stopped—she listened—she almost smiled—
"That sounds like a wail of a motherless child."

A house stood open—no soul was there—
Her dull, tired feet grew light on the stair;
She mounted—entered. One bed on the floor,
And Something in it: and close by the door,
Watching the stark form, stretched out still,
Ignorant knowing not good nor ill,
But only a want and a misery wild,
Crouched the dead mother's motherless child.

What next? Come say what would you have done
Dear children playing about in the sun,
Or sitting by pleasant fireside warm,
Hearing outside the howling storm?
The widow went in and she shut the door,
She stayed by the dead an hour or more—
And when she went home through the night so wild,
She had in her arms a sleeping child.

Now she is old and feeble and dull,
But her empty heart is happy and full
If her crust be hard and her cottage poor
There's a young foot tripping across the floor,

Young hands to help her that never tire,
And a young voice singing beside the fire;
And her tired eyes look as if they smiled,—
Childless mother and motherless child.

The Wren's Nest

I took the wren's nest;—
Heaven forgive me!
Its merry architects so small
Had scarcely finished their wee hall,
That empty still and neat and fair
Hung idly in the summer air.
The mossy walls, the dainty door,
Where Love should enter and explore,
And Love sit caroling outside,
And Love within chirp multiplied;—
I took the wren's nest;—
Heaven forgive me!

How many hours of happy pains
Through early frosts and April rains,
How many songs at eve and morn
O'er springing grass and greening corn,
Before the pretty house was made!
One little minute, only one,
And she'll fly back, and find it—gone!
I took the wren's nest;—
Bird, forgive me!

Thou and thy mate, sans let, sans fear,
Ye have before you all the year,
And every wood holds nooks for you,
In which to sing and build and woo
One piteous cry of birdish pain—
And ye'll begin your life again,
Forgetting quite the lost, lost home
In many a busy home to come—
But I?—Your wee house keep I must
Until it crumble into dust.
I took the wren's nest:
God forgive me!

A Child's Smile

A child's smile—nothing more;
Quiet and soft and grave, and seldom seen,
Like summer lightning o'er,
Leaving the little face again serene.

I think, boy well-beloved,
Thine angel, who did grieve to see how far
Thy childhood is removed
From sports that dear to other children are,

On this pale cheek has thrown
The brightness of his countenance, and made
A beauty like his own—
That, while we see it, we are half afraid,

And marvel, will it stay?
Or, long ere manhood, will that angel fair,
Departing some sad day,
Steal the child-smile and leave the shadow care?

Nay, fear not. As is given
Unto this child the father watching o'er,
His angel up in heaven
Beholds Our Father's face for evermore.

And he will help him bear
His burthen, as his father helps him now;
So he may come to wear
That happy child-smile on an old man's brow.

Over The Hills And Far Away

A little bird flew my window by,
'Twixt the level street and the level sky,
The level rows of houses tall,
The long low sun on the level wall
And all that the little bird did say
Was, "Over the hills and far away."

A little bird sang behind my chair,
From the level line of corn-fields fair,
The smooth green hedgerow's level bound
Not a furlong off—the horizon's bound,
And the level lawn where the sun all day
Burns:—"Over the hills and far away."

A little bird sings above my bed,
And I know if I could but lift my head
I would see the sun set, round and grand,
Upon level sea and level sand,
While beyond the misty distance gray
Is "Over the hills and far away."

I think that a little bird will sing
Over a grassy mound, next spring,
Where something that once was *me*, ye'll leave
In the level sunshine, morn and eve:
But I shall be gone, past night, past day,
Over the hills and far away.

The Two Raindrops

Said a drop to a drop, "Just look at me!
I'm the finest rain-drop you ever did see:
I have lived ten seconds at least on my pane;
Swelling and filling and swelling again.

"All the little rain-drops unto me run,
I watch them and catch them and suck them up each one:
All the pretty children stand and at me stare;
Pointing with their fingers—'That's the biggest drop there.'"

"Yet you are but a drop," the small drop replied;
"I don't myself see much cause for pride:
The bigger you swell up,—we know well, my friend,—
The faster you run down the sooner you'll end.

"For me, I'm contented outside on my ledge,
Hearing the patter of rain in the hedge;
Looking at the firelight and the children fair,—
Whether they look at me, I'm sure I don't care."

"Sir," cried the first drop, "your talk is but dull;
I can't wait to listen, for I'm almost full;
You'll run a race with me?—No?—Then 'tis plain
I am the largest drop in the whole pane."

Off ran the big drop, at first rather slow:
Then faster and faster, as drops will, you know:
Raced down the window-pane, like hundreds before,
Just reached the window-sill—one splash—and was o'er.

The Year's End

So grows the rising year, and so declines
By months, weeks, days, unto its peaceful end
Even as by slow and ever-varying signs
Through childhood, youth, our solemn steps we bend
Up to the crown of life, and thence descend.

Great Father, who of every one takest care,
From him on whom full ninety years are piled
To the young babe, just taught to lisp a prayer
About the "Gentle Jesus, meek and mild,"
Who children loves, being once himself a child,—

O make us day by day like Him to grow;
More pure and good, more dutiful and meek;
Because He loves those who obey Him so;
Because His love is the best thing to seek,
Because without His love, all loves are weak,—

All earthly joys are miserable and poor,
All earthly goodness quickly droops and dies,
Like rootless flowers you plant in gardens—sure
That they will flourish—till in mid-day skies
The sun burns, and they fade before your eyes.

O God, who art alone the life and light
Of this strange world to which as babes we come,
Keep Thou us always children in Thy sight:
Guide us from year to year, thro' shine and gloom
And at our year's end, Father, take us home.

Running After The Rainbow

"Why thus aside your playthings throw,
Over the wet lawn hurrying so?
Where are you going, I want to know?"
"I'm running after the rainbow."

"Little boy, with your bright brown eyes
Full of an innocent surprise,
Stop a minute, my Arthur wise,
What do you want with the rainbow?"

Arthur paused in his headlong race,
Turned to his mother his hot, young face,
"Mother, I want to reach the place
At either end of the rainbow.

"Nurse says, wherever it meets the ground.
Such beautiful things may oft be found
Buried below, or scattered round,
If one can but catch the rainbow.

"O please don't hinder me, mother dear,
It will all be gone while I stay here;"
So with many a hope and not one fear,
The child ran after the rainbow.

Over the damp grass, ankle deep,
Clambering up the hilly steep,
And the wood where the birds were going to sleep,
But he couldn't catch the rainbow.

And when he came out at the wood's far side,
The sun was setting in golden pride,
There were plenty of clouds all rainbow dyed,
But not a sign of the rainbow.

Said Arthur, sobbing, as home he went,
"I wish I had thought what mother meant;
I wish I had only been content,
And not ran after the rainbow."

Miss Mulock

And as he came sadly down the hill,
Stood mother scolding—but smiling still,
And hugged him up close, as mothers will:
So he quite forgot the rainbow.

Dick And I

We're going to a party, my brother Dick and I:
The best, grandest party we ever did try:
And I'm very happy—but Dick is so shy!

I've got a white ball-dress, and flowers in my hair,
And a scarf, with a brooch too, mamma let me wear:
Silk stockings, and shoes with high heels, I declare!

There is to be music—a real soldier's band:
And *I* mean to waltz, and eat ice, and be fanned,
Like a grown-up young lady, the first in the land.

But Dick is so stupid, so silent and shy:
Has never learnt dancing, so says he won't try—
Yet Dick is both older and wiser than I.

And I'm fond of my brother—this darling old Dick:
I'll hunt him in corners wherever he stick,
He's bad at a party—but at school he's a brick!

So good at his Latin, at cricket, football,
Whatever he tries at. And then he's so tall!
Yet at play with the children he's best of us all.

And his going to the party is just to please *me*,
Poor Dick! so good-natured. How dull he will be!
But he says I shall dance "like a wave o' the sea."

That's Shakespeare, his Shakespeare, he worships him so.
Our Dick he writes poems, though none will he show;
I found out his secret, but I won't tell: no, no.

And when he's a great man, a poet you see,
O dear! what a proud little sister I'll be;
Hark! there comes the carriage. We're off, Dick and me.

Grandpapa

Grandpapa lives at the end of the lane,
His cottage is small and its furniture plain;
No pony to ride on, no equipage grand,—
A garden, and just half an acre of land;
No dainties to dine off, and very few toys,—
Yet is grandpapa's house the delight of the boys.

Grandpapa once lived in one little room,
Grandpapa worked all day long at his loom:
He speaks with queer accent, does dear grandpapa,
And not half so well as papa and mamma.
The girls think his clothes are a little rough,
But the boys all declare they can't love him enough.

A man of the people in manners and mind,
Yet so honest, so tender, so clever, so kind:
Makes the best of his lot still, where'er it be cast.
A sturdy old Englishman, game to the last.
Though simple and humble and unknown to fame,
It's good luck to the boys to bear grandpapa's name!

Monsieur Et Mademoiselle.

Deux petits enfants Français,
Monsieur et Mademoiselle.
Of what can they be talking, child?
Indeed I cannot tell.
But of this I am very certain,
You would find naught to blame
In that sweet French politeness—
I wish we had the same.

Monsieur has got a melon,
And scoops it with his knife,
While Mademoiselle sits watching him:
No rudeness here—no strife:
Though could you listen only,
They're chattering like two pies—
French magpies, understand me—
So merry and so wise.

Their floor is bare of carpet,
Their curtains are so thin,
They dine on meagre *potage*, and
Put many an onion in!
Her snow-white caps she irons:
He blacks his shoes, he can;
Yet she's a little lady
And he's a gentleman.

O busy, happy children!
That light French heart of yours,
Would it might sometimes enter at
Our solemn English doors!
Would that we worked as gaily,
And played, yes, played as well,
And lived our lives as simply
As Monsieur et Mademoiselle.

Young Dandelion

Young Dandelion
On a hedge-side,
Said young Dandelion,
"Who'll be my bride?

"I'm a bold fellow
As ever was seen,
With my shield of yellow,
In the grass green.

"You may uproot me,
From field and from lane,
Trample me, cut me,—
I spring up again.

"I never flinch, Sir,
Wherever I dwell;
Give me an inch, Sir.
I'll soon take an ell.

"Drive me from garden
In anger and pride,
I'll thrive and harden
By the road-side.

"Not a bit fearful,
Showing my face,
Always so cheerful
In every place."

Said young Dandelion,
With a sweet air,
"I have my eye on
Miss Daisy fair.

"Though we may tarry
Till past the cold,
Her I will marry
Ere I grow old.

"I will protect her
From all kinds of harm,
Feed her with nectar,
Shelter her warm.

"Whate'er the weather,
Let it go by;
We'll hold together,
Daisy and I.

"I'll ne'er give in,—no!
Nothing I fear:
All that I win, O!
I'll keep for my dear."

Said young Dandelion
On his hedge-side,
"Who'll me rely on?
Who'll be my bride?"

A September Robin

My eyes are full, my silent heart is stirred,
Amid these days so bright
Of ceaseless warmth and light;
Summer that will not die,
Autumn, without one sigh
O'er sweet hours passing by—
Cometh that tender note
Out of thy tiny throat,
Like grief, or love, insisting to be heard,
O little plaintive bird!

No need of word
Well know I all your tale—forgotten bird!
Soon you and I together
Must face the winter weather,
Remembering how we sung
Our primrose fields among,
In days when life was young;
Now, all is growing old,
And the warm earth's a-cold,
Still, with brave heart we'll sing on, little bird,
Sing only. Not one word.